Lily Hollow

a *Bookshop Hotel* novel

A. K. Klemm
with Katie Lavois

grey gecko press

Published by Grey Gecko Press, Katy, Texas.

www.greygeckopress.com

Printed in the United States of America

Library of Congress Cataloging-in-Publication Data
Klemm, A. K.
Lily hollow / A. K. Klemm
Library of Congress Control Number: 201542796
ISBN   978-1-9388219-3-6
First Edition

This book is dedicated to
all those who came before us
and made us who we are

Part One

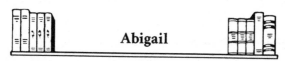

Abigail

Abigail meticulously lined raspberry tarts in the glass case closest to the window facing Main Street and the Bookshop Hotel on the cul-de-sac Aspen Court. She was missing something. She ran her hand from the tarts to the open space. What went to the right? She'd been setting up her baked goods nearly the same way for over fifty years, and today, she couldn't remember how.

She closed her eyes, breathed in, and thought back through the years. When standing here, she remembered Nancy coming through the doors with Sue and Ann nearly every morning. What was in the window? Not muffins. Those stayed in the case near the register. She thought to all the times Jack was across the way, when the Bookshop Hotel was the Lily Hollow Hotel. Cookies? No, those were on the shelves behind the main counter.

She caught a glimpse of Sidney, Jack's granddaughter, climbing into her car on the north side of the bookshop. What was that fool woman up to now? Abigail recalled observing Sidney's daughter, AJ, tramping to the cemetery on similar mornings a year or so back. Ah! Danish rolls next to the tarts. But she'd forgotten to make any today, and that flustered her.

Time was getting away from her. Lots of things were getting away from her. Before, it was just arthritis and achy bones. Now, Abigail felt her mind slipping, and of that she was truly a bit scared.

She spotted Sam on Main Street. But he wasn't headed to the deli, which would be in her direction. He sneaked over to Sidney's car and disappeared into it. Crazy kids. They weren't kids anymore, but sometimes they sure acted like it. Sidney probably thought she had everyone fooled, too. Maybe they did. Maybe it was just Abigail, always peering into everyone's lives through a glass window, who saw Sidney for what she was and what she was always up to.

Sometimes, it felt like she was living on repeat. Tarts, secrets, a couple, a child. Danish rolls, more secrets, a couple, a child. Except all the children were grown, and the Danish rolls were left out of the cycle today. The couples and the secrets kept coming, though, year after year. Sometimes, she found herself seeing the past even when the present was happening in front of her.

Sam

Sam eyed the babysitter with skepticism. She was a redhead, like him, only her hair was an appealing dark auburn while his was closer to carrot. She was chewing bubble gum, and every time her jaw moved, her yellow plastic earrings clanked against her cheek. She was small for her age but nevertheless showed the telltale signs of puberty, and even though he was only seven, Sam couldn't help but think she was pretty.

"Okay, Sam, Mommy will be home in an hour. It's just a quick meeting." Mrs. Finney was aware that she was hovering, but she didn't leave Sam alone often, and Maude's girl seemed too young.

"Mrs. Finney," the girl said, "we'll be fine. We'll play a board game, and you'll be home before it's over."

Mrs. Finney managed a thin, pinched smile. She gave Sam a somewhat desperate hug, and he felt his face squish into her soft curves. Then she was out the door.

"I'm seven, you know," he said defiantly.

"And I'm twelve." She smacked her gum.

"You're too small to be twelve."

"Well, you're too big to be seven."

He cocked his head at her, and a loose red curl fell in front of his eye. Sidney thought how much he looked like a puppy and chuckled to herself.

He narrowed his eyes at her, wondering what was so funny. "What kind of board games do you like?" he asked cautiously.

"I don't. Wanna watch a movie?"

"You told Ma we were gonna play a game."

"You always tell the truth, Sammy?"

"It's Sam."

Sidney had started a leisurely stroll around the living room, running her fingers along the bizarre little knick-knacks and inspecting the odd wall hangings with only marginal interest. "I guess Sammy Finney sounds goofy, doesn't it? I'll call you Sammy-Finns then."

Oh, that's much better, he thought as he shook it off.

"I like Monopoly," he said.

"Monopoly's not a movie."

"If you're going to call me Sammy-Finns, then we're playing Monopoly." Sam stared her down, daring her to argue. She smacked her gum.

"Okay, kid. Monopoly it is."

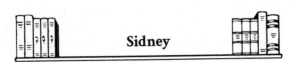

Sidney

Sidney pulled her aging Mercedes into the potholed parking lot at the boutique branch of the local resale outfit in Briar. When people purged their closets of designer label clothing or higher-end costume jewelry, it was more than likely funneled here.

Resale shopping had the potential to be an incredibly depressing venture, filled with screaming children, harsh lighting, and sadly unfashionable clothes, but Sidney found the boutique resale experience to be quite different. It felt more like antiquing than discount shopping. And the jewelry—the jewelry was what drew her here every time she needed to get out of Lily Hollow.

She locked the car and strolled toward the door. As she entered, she was enveloped in cool, musty air. She inhaled deeply and smiled. The shop smelled like aging finery.

"Hi, Jane." Sidney lifted a hand to the slight woman behind the counter.

She looked up from her receipt book and smiled. "Morning, Sidney. You know, we just got a fabulous new lot of earrings in. You better take your pick before they're gone."

"You know I will. But I'm going to look around for a minute first."

Before the woman behind the counter could reply, Sidney disappeared into the clothing racks bunched into the center of the small shop. She almost always made a beeline for the earrings, but she felt a need to browse today. She was moving through the dresses, running her fingers lightly along the hangers and pursing her lips in thought when her breath caught in her throat.

Oh my God, she thought. *That's the one. That's the dress.*

Nearly two weeks had passed since Sam had asked her to marry him. She was still reeling from the fact that she'd said yes, that she'd even thought of saying yes. She was, by all accounts, not the marrying kind and had actually grown fond of the label. She found it glamorous.

Sidney thought of herself as a rather glamorous woman. To those on the outside, she appeared to be a vain and selfish woman who many believed had turned her back on the responsibility that came with real life. In reality, Sidney's true nature lay somewhere in between.

This was the first time since accepting Sam's proposal that she had allowed herself to feel any excitement about the prospect of a wedding. She had found the dress; she knew it. She pulled the dress from the rack and gaped at it. It was simply shaped but form fitting, sheathed in delicate lace that was a hypnotic shade of deep emerald green. A faux-diamond brooch was secured where the fabric gathered below the breast, and dark-green piping radiated from it, wrapping the bodice in pleasing lines. She pressed it to her body and looked down to gauge the fit.

"It suits you."

Sidney's head snapped up, in part because she had been startled, and in part because there was a familiar venom in the voice she heard. Her stomach knotted when she saw the face that belonged to the voice.

"Mrs. Carson," Sidney said coolly as she folded the dress over her arm.

"My apologies for startling you, my dear. I was making a donation and happened to see you across the store." Beverly Carson folded her hands and gave Sidney the rather unsubtle inspection that only the obscenely wealthy can properly execute.

"How nice of you to say hello," Sidney said through a tightening jaw.

"Shopping for a special occasion, Sidney? I seemed to have heard something about you and Marla Finney's son." Mrs. Carson gave Sidney a wry smile. "Will there be a wedding soon?"

"Good news travels fast, it appears," Sidney said before she caught herself. "Although I can't see how it could possibly be of any interest to you."

Mrs. Carson's smile immediately dropped from her face, and her back stiffened. "Sidney, you know our family always had a special interest in you."

Sidney was nearly shaking with anger. "Yes, I suppose you all did . . . eventually."

Sidney sat in her car in front of the Bookshop Hotel, clutching a plastic bag over a hanger and blinking back hot tears.

She still couldn't believe she was living here in her daughter's bookstore—AJ's bookstore. She had to pull herself together before she could go inside and face her. AJ had kept the hotel's suites upstairs as living quarters for her staff, and Sidney had been staying there since her return to Lily Hollow. She checked her face in the visor mirror and lightly wiped the smudges from under her eyes before she made herself get out of the car.

She glanced at the café counter to her left as she entered and felt the vertiginous sensation of the past and present colliding. She stood there holding her future wedding dress and remembered long-lost moments from when this building was nothing more than a rotting pile of trash.

"Ooh, did you find a dress for the gala?" Ivy startled Sidney back to the present as she leaned over the cash wrap area of the bookshop. Sidney heard a thud and turned to see that Ivy had dropped her sketchbook on the floor in an effort to get a peek at the bag.

Sidney must have looked shell-shocked for a moment, because Ivy returned the stare with puzzlement. Sidney looked down at the bundle in her hand, thankful that no one could see what was inside. She was supposed to be shopping for a dress for the gala. How could she have been so stupid? They hadn't told anyone of their wedding plans yet. It was too soon, and AJ was too busy planning what could be a real comeback for this old place. Luckily, Sidney wasn't the type of bride to wear white, so the dress in her arms could be passed off as her gala dress if it came to that.

After hurrying up the back stairway and to the third floor, Sidney jammed her key into the door of 2E and stumbled across the threshold. She closed the door quickly behind her and locked it, crossed the living area to the bed as quickly as she could while ripping the plastic cover away from the hanger, and threw the dress across the comforter. It was perfect, and she couldn't believe her good fortune.

She collapsed into a chair in the corner of her room and looked around her in disbelief. How had she gotten here with these people in this place?

"Hey, Sammy-Finns, you cool to just watch some TV?"

"I guess."

"I'm going to run out. I'll be back. Don't worry, I'll be back before your mom gets home."

Sam shifted in his shoes. They were nearly the same height now. He was big for his age, and she was small for hers. The idea of her being his babysitter had become pretty ridiculous the last couple of years, but it made Mrs. Finney feel better to have someone else at home with him.

"You're a big man. You'll be fine, right?" Sid dropped her hand from the doorknob. She looked at him like she was having second thoughts and wasn't going to leave after all. But he didn't want her to think of him as a kid anymore.

"No, go ahead."

"You're the best." She winked at him and disappeared out the back door.

Sam went to the living room and flipped through the channels. Nothing was on. He shut off the TV and instead turned on the record player. He pulled out an Elvis Costello album and settled on the couch with his hands behind his head, already wondering where Sidney had gone.

Sidney picked her way through town carefully in the dark. Jude liked to make it a challenge, to see how eager she was to meet. While she always chose easy, convenient places, he always made her summon all her skills of stealth and speed just to get a few seconds alone.

They communicated under the radar, never calling each other's homes or even committing anything to paper. He'd place a rock in the garden under the windows at their church if there was a message to seek out. When no one was looking, she'd creep to the window and breathe onto the pane where he would finger something like Rhys6. That told her to meet at the stadium at 6:00. She would wipe away the evidence and pick up the rock if she could meet or leave it behind if she couldn't.

This morning, it had been H83, so she'd picked up the stone knowing she'd be babysitting at the Finney's. Lily Hollow Hotel at 8:30. She checked her watch and saw she had made good time. There were a few scrapes on her legs from bushes snagging her flesh as she picked through gardens and fields, but she'd made it in fifteen minutes.

The floorboards of the old building's porch creaked under her feet, and the smell of rotten wood met her nose as she opened the door. She and Jude had met here once before, but in daylight, in the middle of the afternoon when the sun leaked through the boarded windows and actually made the place look a lot less menacing.

"Jude," she whispered. Her voice started to echo and then fell flat against the dirt and greenery trying to get in through the walls.

She suddenly felt hands on her ass. "Jude Carson!" she said, slapping his hands away, laughing as she turned around. He met her face with a kiss.

"Hi," he said.

"Hi."

"Where have you been all week?"

"Where I always am."

He had his hands up her skirt and kissed her again. "You know, there are rooms upstairs."

"I'm not going up there. Those stairs are falling apart."

He tugged at her underwear. "There's a counter in the kitchen." The idea of having sex on the dirty kitchen counter of a condemned hotel didn't sound very romantic, but Jude was already tugging at his own pants. They had been making out for months, but this was the first time he'd actually made a move to take it any further. He seemed desperate and hungry, and Sidney liked giving him what he wanted.

Sidney also liked walking around town with a secret. The secret that Jude Carson could probably have any girl in Lily Hollow, but it was her he kept leaving messages for. It was her he wanted to see. In a town full of girls who were in love with him, she was the one who knew what his lips and hands felt like. It was Sidney whom he met in dark places in between classes at the high school. Sidney loved hearing the other girls in class talking about Jude with his corn-silk hair and unbelievably blue eyes. She liked thinking, *You have no idea*.

But now, in this moment, she wondered why he was so secretive about his affection. Why was he only hers in the dark? The thought made her hesitate.

Jude picked her up and set her on the counter and kissed her hard again.

"We don't have much time," she said, thinking the statement would slow him down and make him wait for later. It only made him more desperate. He climbed up on the counter with her and pulled her shirt off.

"I love you," she said hopefully.

"Me, too."

And that was it. It was over before it really began.

She immediately thought of Granddaddy Jack and how disappointed he would be to know she desecrated his old hotel with her sin.

"I've got to go," she said, putting her shirt back on.

Jude looked stunned, equally guilty. "I—wha—Sid."

"It's okay, I won't tell anyone." The words were out of her mouth before she had thought about it. She kissed his mouth to cover up the awkwardness between them. "I still love you," she reassured him and then ran out of the hotel, trying not to let him see the tears that had started to spill down her burning cheeks.

She cried all the way back to the Finneys', and when Sam let her in the back door, she swore he could see the change in her. *It won't matter if I don't tell. Everyone will see it.*

"Mom will be here in ten," Sam said, feeling contempt for Sidney for the first time.

"Oh, okay."

"Why are you out of breath?"

"I ran."

"Whatever."

"Sammy . . ."

"Just next time, get me a Coke or something. Mom never lets me have them."

But there wasn't a next time.

In all of Sidney's memories, it was Jude's smell and the smell of the hotel she remembered most. Though he was the grandson of a pastor, he was not much different from the other boys at the high school, but his scent was.

His mother washed everything in ylang ylang oil, a flower that, when mixed with homemade rolled cigarettes and mashed cloves, reminded Sidney of an exotic, far-off place. As if that wasn't enough, his hair always smelled like he'd been rolling in a field of clovers. And, in fact, sometimes he had. On more than one occasion, he and Sidney had snuck out under the bleachers in a bed of the purple flowers and other weeds to skip class and share a smoke. She never did get the grass stains out of those jeans. She had been sentimental and let them sit too long before washing them.

Her mother had eyed them with knowing irritation but said nothing. Sidney figured if her mother knew enough to reprimand her, then she must have done the same thing at some point and therefore had no right to reprimand.

"You've been up to something, young lady," Maude would say.

"Yes, Mama. Lots of somethings. With lots of someones."

It wasn't until later that Sidney truly realized what a comment like that could imply.

When she started throwing up, Maude innocently said, "You probably got that kissing disease."

Sidney didn't know what the kissing disease was, but she felt the color drain from her cheeks and the dizziness set in. "Yes, Mama." She tried sarcasm. "I'm pregnant." But the words fell flat. She recognized the moment she spoke that the words rang true.

Maude looked at Sidney in disbelief.

"Sidney, that's not funny."

Sidney said nothing and looked at her feet. Horrified, Maude grabbed her by the shoulders and shook her, shrieking, "Are you pregnant?"

"Maybe." Her answer sounded more like a question.

Maude let her go and sank to the floor, crying silent, disturbed tears.

Sidney expected yelling or worrisome meddling. Instead, Maude barely managed to whisper, "With who?"

"I don't know, Ma. Could be anyone!" Sidney screamed in frustration. How could that be the first question? How could that be all she cared about? Did it matter whose it was? And why? Maude had never taken a genuine interest in Sidney's friends before. Besides, Jude didn't know, and she wasn't about to let him find out in Sunday school.

That night at the hotel had been rushed, and Sidney had forgotten to slip the stone into Jude's letterman jacket so he could summon her again. She was sure that all they needed to do was talk. He loved her, after all—he said he did. At church on Sunday, she tossed the rock under their window and waited. He walked by, glanced at it, and then glanced back at her but kept going.

He played with the hair across his forehead all during the service that day. Sidney tapped her shoes against the pew, and Maude flicked her fingernails. Sidney decided she couldn't tell. She wouldn't tell. Whether he deserved it or not, Sidney decided to protect him.

"I don't know what you're trying to pull," Maude told her, "but not holding him accountable to his responsibilities isn't doing anyone any favors. Not him, not you, and surely not that baby."

Sidney's belly was huge by then, and that's when the real lectures began. Those were the months Sidney spent at home being stubborn. That's when Sidney stopped calling her "Mama" and "Ma" for the most part. The sounds of the words dried up in her throat, knowing some-one would have to use them on her soon.

Ironically, the one she'd feared disappointing the most, her grand-father, was the only one capable of mustering a smile. Granddaddy Jack gave her a hug and promised her it would all turn out okay.

Miss Abigail came over a lot, having midwifed with her mother a few times over the years. "That man always did get excited over a new baby," Abigail said one day.

Granddaddy Jack smiled proudly and took to rubbing Sidney's belly when Maude wasn't around to scold him for encouraging her state of affairs.

Sidney hoped Jude wouldn't take her lead on the silent act. She thought if he saw how nicely she kept a secret to protect him, he would reward her by coming forward. Maybe they could get married in the church and be a family—not right away, but one day. But who was she kidding? Jude took the out and never did visit or say a word.

Sidney came home from school exhausted and brain dead. She'd been up all night with AJ, trying to get her to sleep only to have the wig-gly baby refuse. Around four o'clock in the morning, Maude groggily came into her room, snatched the baby away, and cradled her in her arms.

"Do you know how to do anything, Sidney, except make every-one miserable?"

Sidney might have bothered to argue if the child hadn't instantly quieted, nestling down in her grandmother's bony arms. She heard the back screen door slam and Maude sit down in the creaky rocking chair on the back porch facing the garden. Granddaddy Jack had roses and tomatoes that ran rampant all around the yard. Sidney's grand-mother Emma had planted them in neat rows when they first bought the house, but after she died, Granddad only pulled weeds. He didn't have the heart to trim back anything that might have been Emma's.

Cool air came in through Sidney's own open window, and the creaking of Maude's chair lulled her to sleep. She'd forgotten to do her homework.

Homework didn't matter anymore. After she became "the pregnant girl," no one expected much out of her. Most teachers were too busy praising the college-bound students to bother reprimanding the teen mom. That was all well and good with Sidney except for how lonesome it got. She spent the better half of her lunch periods smoking under the bleachers.

"Isn't that bad for the kid or something? You know, smoking when you're, you know . . ." Carol Maxwell jabbed at Sidney's breasts.

"She's got formula. I'm not too keen on having a kid suck off my tits before I'm even twenty."

Carol took a drag off her cigarette. "No kidding. So glad it wasn't me."

Sidney didn't answer. She'd say she wished it hadn't been her, but she loved AJ. Sure, it was hard having a screaming, pooping child on your hands while everyone else was out being a teenager, but the party scene in Lily Hollow wasn't really much to brag about, and AJ would be someday. She held her cigarette and smiled silently to herself as warm pride washed over her.

The bell rang, and Carol got to her feet, flicking her smoke to the pavement. "Time to get a move on," she said.

"Yep," Sidney replied as her smiled faded. They shuffled back inside to finish the day.

Later, standing in the doorway of the house, Sid dropped her bags on the floor and wanted to go to her room and nap, but Maude handed her the baby and started cleaning the house.

"She's hungry now."

AJ stretched her feet out, wiggled her toes into the crook of Sidney's arm, squirmed, farted, and laughed. The fart sounded too wet to just be a fart, and the laugh turned to tears far too quickly. Sidney grimaced in disgust.

"Sidney!" Maude shouted. "Go change her diaper!"

"Yeah. Right." She sighed, carrying AJ to her bedroom, where she changed her diaper.

It had probably been about an hour when Sidney woke up, realizing that she had fallen asleep instead of feeding the baby. She stumbled into the kitchen only to find Abigail Lacey, instead of her mother, holding the baby.

"Don't worry, Maude thinks you were doing homework. She's napping. The baby is fed. Jack is writing."

Where Maude was stiff and bony—a taller woman who had taken after her father—Abigail was soft. Sidney often wondered why Granddaddy Jack had married Emma, a woman who was more of a concept than a person to her.

"You're a saint, Abigail," Sidney said as she started making a peanut butter sandwich. The old woman beamed.

"I used to hold you like this," she said, brushing a tuft of hair away from the baby's eyebrow as she slept. "And Maude."

"Why didn't you have your own babies, Abigail?"

"I never married."

"Ha! Obviously, that didn't stop me."

"Sidney!"

"Well, it's true."

Granddaddy Jack came in then. "I thought I smelled an open jar of peanut butter." Sidney had left it open on the counter, and Jack picked it up and stuck his finger right in and scooped out a finger full. "Mmmm, mmmm, that stuff never gets old."

"Peanut butter?"

"This is peanut butter from the MacGregor market," he corrected her. "During the war, peanut butter sandwiches were on military rations, but it didn't taste like this. And then there were times when I couldn't have it at all." When his finger was licked clean, he took the baby from Abigail's arms and draped AJ right over his shoulder, this baby who belonged to everybody and nobody.

"Well, I guess I'll go do my homework for real this time," Sidney said. But when she got to her room, she just sat on her bed and stared out the window. Jude Carson was walking up the road, swinging a stick. She willed him to set a course for the front door and declare himself the father of her child, but all he managed to do was slow his pace while he passed her house. Or maybe she imagined his change in pace. She was too scared to open the window and call out to him.

What if someone heard? Or worse, what if he ignored her? She wanted to chase after him or throw stones and scream. That would be satisfying, she mused, throwing the very stones from the church garden right at his head.

But she didn't do any of those things. Instead, she sat there frozen on her bed staring after him as the sun began to set. White blue jeans and white shirt, he looked like Apollo walking under the glow of the low sun like that. It was surreal, looking at him at a distance and thinking he'd fathered her child.

When he was gone, Sidney curled into a bit of a ball and closed her eyes, praying she could just blink into another reality. That she could be someone else, even if it were for a few moments. It was times like this that she would tell herself that one day, no one would know the circumstances of her pregnancy. One day, baby AJ would be a grown person, and Sidney would be too old to be constantly reminded of her mistakes.

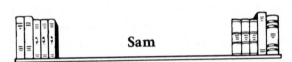

Sam

Sam carried the tray of sandwiches across Main Street. The metal pan was stretched across his right shoulder, loaded with layers of carefully wrapped deli fare. He had always been a large guy, and he now had this morning ritual down pat, so the tray was fairly easy to manage. He'd been delivering a select menu from his deli across the street to the Bookshop Hotel every morning since it opened. His girlfriend's daughter owned and ran the place, and over the last few years, it had become a bit of a local community center.

He felt the slightest little drip drop and sprinkle of rain drizzle down on his nose, and he squinted up to the sky. The clouds were rolling in over Lily Hollow, and it looked like there might be a solid rain coming on. Well, that would spoil his plans. He was thinking about taking Sidney out for a walk, probably down by MacGregor Bridge.

It was pretty out there, a lot of trees, a lot of stunning but out-of-place granite, and the creek with a small four-foot waterfall. He was hoping that some alone time with Sidney might help soften her to the idea of getting married. Sidney didn't like the idea of being tied down, and so far, any discussion of the topic had sent her edging in the opposite direction.

"What if you got tired of me?" she'd asked. "Why can't we just live together first?"

That's just not the way things are done! Sam had wanted to yell.

If you love a guy, you stick around. If you love a guy, you don't plan for the relationship to fail. If you love a guy, you don't run around acting like a mistress. You become his wife.

But Sidney never did what most women did. Most men he knew talked about their girlfriends or wives in a nostalgic haze. "I miss when it was easy." Easy? Relationships? It was never easy with Sidney. He didn't know if others he knew had a knack for rewriting history or if Sidney was just that difficult, so difficult that nothing had ever been easy with them—ever. But somehow, for some reason, she'd said yes when he'd asked her to marry him.

Now he spotted her in the window of the old Victorian estate. The rain was starting to come down harder, and he motioned for her to let him in. The servant's entrance around back that he usually used was far more exposed. He didn't want the sandwiches getting damp.

"Open the door, Sid!" he yelled from the sidewalk.

"No!" she shouted back. "I just mopped, and I'm not mopping twice!"

He groaned and headed to the back where Matthew, the assistant manager of the bookstore, held the door open.

"Sorry, man," Matthew said, taking the tray from Sam as he entered.

"Stubborn woman," Sam grumbled. He shook out his red curls, bits of rainwater flinging off his head.

Sidney came around the corner of the kitchen entrance, carrying a mop and a bucket. "Oh, stop your whining. I told you I just mopped the floor, and if AJ is going to put me to work as a glorified janitor, I'm only doing my work once!"

"You're not the janitor," Matthew said. "She just wanted you to clean up your own mess."

"My mess!"

"Yes, your bottle of wine. Your little party with Ivy in the bookstore last night. Your mess."

Sidney waved Matthew away and kissed Sam's wet cheek. "I'm sorry you got wet."

Sam knew this was more of her way to change the subject and dismiss Matthew and not really an apology at all. "Not sorry enough to open the door for me next time," he said.

"Nope. Not a bit." She winked and smiled as she turned away from him and back to her mop.

At that, Sid's daughter, AJ, came down the stairs, and Matthew instinctively handed her a coffee mug.

Sam smiled and said, "What a family we make."

"Mmm, yes," AJ said.

At the same time, Sidney responded, "We're not family." Sam saw that she realized she'd spoiled a moment, and she quickly asked, "Are we?"

The woman had such funny ideas about family and how they were supposed to function. She'd left home and let her mother and grandfather raise her daughter, and only recently—now that AJ was fully grown and more than capable—came back to be involved. Instead of being motherly, Sidney had spent AJ's childhood seeing what the rest of the world had to offer. Somehow, it was all coming together again, and Sam knew it was only a matter of time before Sidney acknowledged reality. This was her family, and it was a good thing.

AJ sipped her coffee as Matthew busied himself with emptying the sandwich tray into the fridge. Sidney looked as though she were waiting for something. Direction? Praise? Who knew? Sam made a move to leave but lingered in the door frame, taking up its entire space and managing to look both impressively sturdy and awkward at the same time.

"You need something else?" Sid asked.

"No. I just . . . You look nice."

"Aww. Thanks." She blew a strand of hair out of her face as he turned to leave.

"Oh, and Abigail never opened up this morning," he said.

"We'll go check on her," AJ called after him.

Of course, outside, it was a complete downpour. He didn't even try to hurry; it wouldn't keep him any drier.

When Sidney's daughter had officially announced her engagement to Kevin Rhys, Sam had grimaced. It wasn't that he didn't like the idea—

he really did love those kids. He just wondered if Sidney would actually come home to see her daughter's wedding, and his grimace was more a combination of anticipation and dread. The thought of her missing it ate at him, and the thought of her coming tied his stomach in knots.

As it happened, he spotted Sidney in the back of the park at the wedding. She looked exotic and slightly bored. Thin, purple material held her upper body snug and fell loose as it draped down, licking her legs. Sure, it was cute when he was a kid, having the hots for his babysitter—a cute cliché even—but now, as an adult, he could see he had not been wrong.

Every man in Lily Hollow was sneaking glances back at Sidney Montgomery, especially Jude Carson. And it wasn't because they were gawking at the woman who had once been a teen mom. They were appreciating her and all her wiles.

She was lying low, though, trying not to make a scene. Or trying not to be seen, rather. But Sidney—though sneaky enough—had never really been good at being invisible. Chandelier earrings tickled her neck and threatened to get tangled up in that luscious hair. She'd always loved her earrings. He used to help her pick them out at the thrift store with the money she'd earned from babysitting him. The thought of it made Sam darken with embarrassment. To this day, he still felt as though he could follow her anywhere.

Sam waited until the wedding was over and approached her at the reception. Her mouth was full of one of his sandwiches, and she turned to Maude and said, "Oh my God, these are so good."

"Thanks," Sam said.

Sidney half choked on the sandwich. "Sammy-Finns. You're all grown up." She acted surprised, but it hadn't been that long since she'd caught a glimpse of him. A few years back, she'd even popped into the deli briefly. Sam's mother had been there that day, though, and Sid had just popped right back out again. But he was sure she had seen him.

What was she playing at?

Maude walked away to talk to the in-laws, and Sidney brushed her hand against the back of his.

"So Sam, how's life?"

"Good."

"Got a girlfriend?"

"Nope."

"Interesting."

They spent the entire reception not bumping into each other. She made eyes at him across the lawn, only for him to notice her looking away from Jude Carson moments later. Finally, Jude disappeared, and evening set in.

The newlyweds were long gone, and most of the guests had left. Maude and Mrs. Rhys seemed to be lone janitors, picking up trash and organizing the chairs from opposite sides of the park.

Sidney leaned against a tree and lit a cigarette, which looked like the last one of an entire pack smoked that day. It was dusk, and two owls swooped back and forth, darting at unseen creatures in the grass. High in the tree Sidney had melted into, Sam could see the silhouette of a nest against the gray sky. He walked over to her and leaned against the tree, too, his elbow tugging on a strand of hair near her shoulder.

"Need a smoke, Sammy-Finns?"

"I don't smoke, Sidney."

"Good," she said around the cigarette. "I don't have any but the one in my mouth."

"So if I'd said yes, were you planning to share?"

She sucked in and pulled the cigarette away from her mouth, letting the smoke roll out slowly across her lips as an answer.

"Want to get out of here?" he asked.

"That's a very grown-up question, Sammy-Finns."

"I suppose it is."

He woke up in her hotel room alone. She'd checked out and called a taxi without waking him or saying goodbye.

Sam showered and made the bed, even though he knew a maid would come in and tear it apart to wash the sheets. He was angry. Angry at himself. Angry at her. Angry at the fact that he was in his thirties and still lived with his mother, who would know he hadn't come home.

The smell of Sidney's perfume hung in the air. Even though it was a non-smoking room, he could tell she'd opened the window and had a cigarette before leaving. She'd forgotten to relock the window, and even though he was hurt, a smile touched his lips for a mere second as he snapped the lock shut.

He didn't see her again until she showed up at the Bookshop Hotel after AJ had restored the old building.

AJ

The Bookshop Hotel had a full-swing gala in the works, and AJ was a little more than terrified that maybe she'd bitten off more than she could chew. She'd first conceived of the idea nearly a year and a half ago and had intended to have it the very next June. Well, that June had come and passed, and they'd still not been ready for an event of that magnitude.

Now it was creeping up on April of the following year, and the invitations were sitting in the downstairs office, awaiting their addresses and stamps. It had taken longer than she'd anticipated to hunt down all the old families, but Matthew had been a great help as always. The entertainment was booked, the flowers for the centerpieces had been ordered from MacGregor Nurseries, and she'd even ordered a tux for Matthew and a dress for herself.

Years ago, AJ had been married, and her husband had died young. She'd had neither the privilege nor the responsibility of planning her wedding or his funeral. Suddenly, she found herself caught up in the excitement of a large-scale event—not just the small-town parties she'd planned for the shop so far, but an affair with live music, evening wear, flowers, and proper invitations. She was married to this bookstore now, and this gala was the wedding she'd never had a chance to plan.

She climbed the stairs to the fourth floor—the forgotten floor above the bookshop, above the living quarters she'd filled with her new family, above the whole world, it seemed. AJ looked out a small peephole-style window in the hall that faced the front of 32 Aspen

Court. She surveyed the Green in the center of the cul-de-sac and looked across the property to Main Street. She could just see the strip center and Sam's Deli, and her stomach rumbled for a sandwich.

"Hey." Matthew rested his chin on her shoulder and spoke quietly into her ear.

"How's it going?" She settled back into his chest, and he moved his chin to the top of her head.

"The woodwork is all done, and the sawdust has been swept away. Want to come see?"

"Yes." She couldn't stop the smile from stretching across her face. He took her hand and opened the first door.

The room was clean and clear, and built-in shelves and filing drawers lined the walls. The boxes of her great-granddaddy Jack's archives and files that were once stashed haphazardly in a mountain of chaos were now stacked neatly in the center of the room.

"Those are the boxes we've already gone through," Matthew said. "We just have to file them. Into those." He pointed to the built-in filing cabinets, and AJ nearly did a tap dance before her bad leg stopped her from celebrating to her fullest desires. "Go on, I know you want to." He smiled at her.

"But we had dinner plans."

"I can bring dinner up if you want."

"Really?"

"Sure, after you see the rest."

"There's more?"

"Of course there's more. What do you think I've been doing up here for months on end?"

"Enjoying the solace?" She giggled.

"Not a chance."

They went to the next room. AJ noticed he'd polished up the room numbers. 3A, 3B . . . "Oh!" she gasped. The suites were fixed up like the ones on the floor below.

"We can't house the whole guest list, obviously, but we'll be able to have rooms available for at least one floor of gala attendees. The rest will have to stay in Briar or Garvin, but we'll be able to house a few."

"Thank you, Matthew."

He kissed the back of her head. "Of course. And you're welcome."

She had pulled an all-nighter worthy of her college days, putting all the files into cabinets with care. Just like alphabetizing, putting guest books and receipts in chronological order had its charm and served as a catharsis.

But now, in the bright light of the afternoon, and despite her third cup of coffee, she was having a hard time keeping her eyes open as she hand wrote all the addresses. Ivy was happily stamping away, having been taken off addressing duty because she kept dawdling over it, adding ornate calligraphy and flair to each letter when there wasn't time to do so.

Matthew dropped a latte on the table and sped away to greet a customer at the door. AJ rubbed her temples, trying to keep the names on the paper from blurring. Her head throbbed a bit, and she heard Sidney and Sam come in through the kitchen entrance. They sounded like they were arguing about something again. She groaned and thought to herself that those two took the whole passionate-redhead stereotype to a completely different level. And to think, she'd always appreciated Sam for his calm, collected attitude.

She blocked out her mother and Sam and stared at the names again. "Peter Pendritch, what a nice name. Ivy, can you read that address for me? My eyes are starting to burn."

"Seriously, you should just go take a nap. 4009 Hollyway, Briar. Oh look, one in Briar. Surely he'll come."

"Thank you, Ivy." AJ scrawled the name across the envelope. It wasn't beautiful calligraphy like Ivy could do, but there was something to be said about an old-fashioned handwritten address on an envelope. She thought the older generations she was inviting to the gala would appreciate that, too.

"Well, Peter Pendritch," Ivy said to the envelope, "we cannot wait to have your acquaintance. Or would you say make your acquaintance? Meet your acquaintance?"

"Ivy, stop talking to the envelopes."

"Why? It keeps you awake."

AJ took Mr. Pendritch's invitation from Ivy's hand and added it to the ever-growing pile. For a second, she thought the name sounded familiar, but of course it might. He'd been living in Briar for longer than she'd been alive. Surely someone knew him. Maybe Abigail, even. She'd have to remember to ask.

An hour later, they were done, and she passed the bundle to Ivy. "Take these to the post office for me?"

"And you'll go take a nap?"

"Yes," AJ said, relieved. "I am dying to take a nap. I just really wanted those done."

Matthew walked by and kissed her forehead. "Go! Nap!"

Anyone who has ever been a reader (or had to share a bed with one) knows that no matter how tired you are, you can't really fall asleep without first trying to read yourself to sleep. More than anything, it's the act of clutching the book in your hands that soothes you to slumber, like an infant with a baby blanket or small stuffed animal.

Even after staying up all night filing and then working well into the mid-afternoon addressing invitations, AJ was unable to just crawl in bed and take a nap like a normal human. Instead, she crawled under the sheets, grabbed her book off the nightstand, and, burning eyes and all, opened up the authorized biography of Roald Dahl called *Storyteller*. Dahl was fascinating, and despite his being a man who'd hated biographies, AJ found herself completely taken in with his.

Matthew poked his head into room. "Cheater. We gave you nap time, not reading time."

"Hey, who's the boss?"

He climbed into bed with her, and she settled into his shoulder, propping the book up on his chest so she could still see the words on the pages.

"If you're up here, who's downstairs?"

"Sidney."

"Is that a good idea? I thought I heard her and Sam fighting earlier. I don't want her brooding at the counter."

"Nah, they made up. They always do."

"Thank you for not fighting with me." AJ turned her head to his chest and kissed his T-shirt.

"Don't worry, I will when it matters."

AJ laughed a little. "Well, thank you for not fighting with me when it doesn't matter." She snuggled into his arms and continued to read—well, half read and half contemplated her mother. She was tired, and it was hard to focus, so her thoughts reverted back to the one person who had always been simultaneously there and not there.

Her mother defined so much of who she was by her mere absence, and now that Sidney was around, AJ found herself grateful and frustrated at the same time. She expected her to flee at any moment, but somehow, she knew she wouldn't. AJ was constantly surprised by the person her mother really was, this last year proving that, in every way imaginable, she was subtly different from what AJ had grown up believing.

She thought back to her great-grandfather, who she adored, and began to question his motives and his ideas, because AJ knew now that it was his urging that had sent Sidney packing all those years ago. Growing up, she'd believed that it was something gone wrong between her and Maude, but Maude—though a bit cold and indifferent at times—was a hard worker, and that included working hard at relationships. Maude would have fought for her daughter if she'd known how, if she hadn't been hindered.

Oh, what did AJ know? She hadn't been there. And Granddaddy Jack had always been a saint to her. Why drag his memory through the mud now?

Because Sidney was in love with Sam. Anyone could see that.

But Sidney didn't know how to sit still. Sidney didn't know how to love.

When AJ went to turn the page, she craned her neck a bit to look at Matthew's face and found that he had fallen asleep. *Nap shark*, she thought.

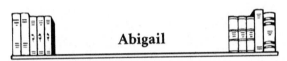

Abigail

It was late afternoon, and Abigail had left the bakery for the day to come sift through old photographs with AJ. AJ had dragged a large number of albums downstairs to the café and was pumping Abigail for stories—if she could remember any—from events in the pictures. Seeing pictures wasn't enough to recreate the ambiance of old parties and weddings; she wanted to *feel* the pictures.

Abigail enjoyed talking more now that she was older, especially around AJ. It was somehow a little bit safer to speak with Jack gone. She thought that maybe AJ sensed what Abigail felt, that the end was near and there was wisdom to pass on. Of course, AJ masked these meetings with coffee and plans for the gala, but Abigail suspected that AJ was humoring an old lady before she lost her forever.

"I forgot to put the tarts in the oven yesterday," Abigail confessed.

"I forgot to put all the online orders in the post last week. We're getting old together." AJ laughed.

"No, dear, you don't understand. I haven't forgotten to put tarts in the oven in—well, almost never. The day Evie died, I didn't, but it wasn't so much I forgot as I just didn't do it. I flew out of the kitchen and ran is all."

AJ then realized the severity of what Abby was telling her. When she hadn't showed up to open the bakery, it wasn't because of the rain or because she'd slept in. She'd forgotten. Abigail had actually lost track of not just time but her duties. What if AJ hadn't sent Sidney to get her? She'd been worried about the storm, knowing how old that house of hers was. AJ wanted Abby at the Hotel, because it was solid and ancient and there were plenty of places to hide safely.

"This time, I plumb forgot," Abby continued. "I thought I'd break a hip, fall down some stairs, you know. Or maybe even get the cancer. I never thought my mind would go like Mama's and Ollie's. We always thought it was the war that did it to him, and I suppose with Mama, I just didn't think. But I guess it wasn't the war. I never connected the dots, AJ. And I'm alone, all alone. Jack's gone."

"It's okay, Abby. We're here." AJ didn't know who Ollie was, and Abigail recognized this in her expression. Of course she didn't know. She'd never mentioned Uncle Ollie before. Why would she? She supposed he'd never been relevant until now. It occurred to her then that AJ didn't know any of them. Not Mama and Ollie, not Evie, and without knowing Evie, you couldn't really know Jack.

Jack had been Abigail's rock her whole life. Maybe they had never married. Maybe his children were hers only in spirit. But Jack and Abigail had been longtime partners, cohorts facing the world together. That selfish man hadn't just sat around being loved by her his whole life. He'd gone and died first, too. Now Abigail was facing her worst imaginable end, losing her mind while all of Jack's secrets were tied up inside her, little demons wanting to break loose of their chains.

"We'll have to get my recipes on paper," Abigail said as she stared away from AJ and out the window, hoping to conceal the bright, hot fear that suddenly washed over her. Recipes would keep the rest at bay. They always kept her calm and kept her mind clear.

"Yes."

"I need to train someone. You can't keep the Bookshop Hotel café running without Abigail's Bakery across the street. And don't tell me you can. I don't want to hear it." At this, Abigail gathered herself and turned to AJ.

"No, we can't do it without Abigail's," AJ agreed, patting her favorite elderly lady on the hand.

The woman sighed and offered a weak and tired smile.

"You know, Abby, Granddaddy Jack left money for your care and funeral arrangements in the will."

"He would think to bury me." Abigail laughed, though she was relieved by the knowledge that she wouldn't be a burden on anyone, at least not entirely.

"Well, that's not coming yet," AJ said, "I just thought you should know. He loved you, and . . ."

"Don't. It's all water under the bridge." Quite literally, actually. Under the MacGregor Bridge.

Abigail remembered standing in the rain on the road to the bridge, her dress clinging to her. When she'd caught a reflection of herself in the window of the car as it had pulled up, she'd found herself thinking, *My oh my, how I look like Evie.*

It was the dress slinking against her skin with the wet.

"I saw these gala invitations!" Nancy Harrigan entered the shop waving an invitation above her pink hat. Nancy had always sported smart business suits, even when she was a girl, Abigail remembered. Lately, though, the woman had taken up hats.

"Hello, Nancy." AJ smiled. Abigail offered a little smile and nod as well.

"What are we reading this quarter?" AJ asked. Nancy ran a ladies' book club—inspired by AJ, naturally—that was hosted by the Bookshop Hotel. Abigail made special treats that matched the theme of the book every month. The ladies had been trying to get her to join in and read as well, but Abigail had never cared to read that much. She read, but only when it suited her. Years ago, she would have joined in just to please them, but now she lost her place and concentration too quickly and couldn't get beyond a few pages before she forgot what she was up to.

"Barbara Kingsolver, Kate Morton, Edna St. Vincent Millay, and a Bronte, as you recommended," Nancy said. "Don't change the subject." She waved the invitation above her head again for emphasis.

"Sounds like an excellent quarter," AJ said and smiled at Abigail. Just like Jack when she did that. Lately, the twinkle Abigail missed from Jack's face and eyes was appearing in AJ's. He was gone, and Abigail had half a mind to believe that the twinkle had left him and inserted itself in AJ's lovely eyes as his soul left this world. *Do you suppose that's how people get their twinkles?* Abigail wondered. *From the souls of those who have passed?* It sounded so whimsical, like something Evie would have speculated.

"I'm sure it will be. Now about this gala!" Nancy would not be distracted.

"It's already in full swing."

"I want to help."

"But Nancy, you're a guest. I don't want—"

"*I'm* helping." Abigail was feeling mischievous all of a sudden and tripped up the conversation that AJ was certain to manipulate.

Nancy pounced. "She's a guest, and she's helping. Please, I want to help. It would mean so much," she pressed.

AJ looked hard at the two women who just ganged up on her. She couldn't blame them. Everyone wanted a piece of the action, and AJ had been protecting the plans for the event like a mother hen. She really wanted Nancy to kick back and enjoy herself. She wanted Abigail to reminisce in a healthy way.

Years ago, Nancy had been married here. Abigail had seen this place as so many things. This gala was for them and an entire generation of women and men who had married and vacationed, partied, and even one who'd had a baby here.

"All right," AJ said. Abigail winked at Nancy, and AJ continued speaking. "Everything indoors is settled. Even the gardens are taken care of, but if you want to really help, I have a dream for the Green that I was going to leave out until now."

Nancy's eyes brightened, and she grabbed a chair to join them at the table. AJ opened a yellowed album to a page marked with Post-It note.

Nancy took in the image and sighed. Abigail saw the picture and remembered seeing it framed in the town hall years ago. It was a photograph taken by a journalist who was present the night of the party that took down the building at 31 Aspen Court. It was a party so grand that the building on the hotel's right (left from the street view) had burned to the ground.

White lights and party tents lit up the Green. The photograph was an old black and white, but it captured the images of other photographers snapping shots of patrons as they posed on the Green.

"This album is full of those photos. I want them set out on tables for people to see."

"I know exactly what you want," Nancy said.

Abigail smiled at them both and said in an excited, childish voice, "I found a diamond ring in the rubble!"

Matthew

Matthew was exhausted. He'd been working night and day on the third and fourth floors. With it near completion, he could now focus on all the work he still had to do on the first floor. They were expanding their rare books and antiquities selection. What had originally been an office was slowly being eaten by that growing section of the store. AJ wanted—and Matthew agreed—for all the space on the first floor to essentially be customer space.

There was no need for an office downstairs when she had so many rooms above her for filing and processing. That's why it had begun as a reading room, with antiquities spread throughout the upper levels in their appropriate sections. Then AJ bought the entire collection of a collector in Michigan upon his death, and the bookstore found itself in need of some change. Matthew started to understand that bookstores, no matter how quaint and homey, are always in flux. The inventory today is not the same inventory tomorrow.

It worked out well that AJ was able to bring some focus to the whimsical feel of this gala with a rare book room, a.k.a. the George Edelstein Collection reveal. While he was doing handiwork and construction, she was sitting all day with lighter fluid, erasers, and other book-cleaning tools preparing special signed copies for presentation.

With little to no sleep every day, Matthew had begun to love early morning. He wasn't naturally a morning person and didn't wake easily, but it was hard to say no to them here when he had projects at hand and the smell of fresh coffee wafting from the kitchen. In the early mornings, he got the espresso machine warmed up and ready for the day, went through the methodical routine of preparing the French press, and spent at least one cup alone on the back stoop listening to the nature that enveloped the hotel before finally drifting upstairs to wake AJ and start his work on the fourth floor.

Many mornings, he didn't have to get AJ. She made her way to the kitchen and sat with him for his second cup and a small breakfast. In the winter, he often got the fireplace going in the café, and they planned their day in front of it.

Life with AJ was easy and comfortable, which made Sidney and Sam's slightly volatile relationship all the more stressful. When you've found yourself in a simple, comfortable existence, other people's turmoil can be a surprisingly disruptive force. He used to handle the chaos of the big city and a semi-psychotic girlfriend, but he had since lost his taste for hassle and drama. Still, it baffled him that Sam and Sidney's drama was so disruptive to him now. Hearing an argument in the distance when he was sleepily watching the sun come up wasn't a big deal, but it was disconcerting that his quiet mornings were no more.

He tried to shield AJ from it as much as he could. She was so excited about this gala and so focused on the Edelstein inventory, he wanted her brain there, not trying to keep track of whether Sam and Sid were on the outs again. In the grand scheme of things, knowing about every little spat was pretty irrelevant, as they did always end up together again after a few days. Somehow, two very good people appeared to have an uncanny ability to bring out the worst in each other. Yet . . .

They were changing, both of them. Sam had been quietly talking about trying to find his own place. He had plenty of money saved up from years of owning his own business and sharing an inexpensive mortgage with his mother. Mrs. Finney's mortgage would be paid off in a few months, and he thought maybe it was time to buy his own house outright in cash before he and Sidney got married. Matthew had also noticed that Sidney was being more reliable around the shop for a change. She might grumble about her part of the work, and she might give them a lot of hell about it, but she was getting it done, and she hadn't left them high and dry yet.

To be honest, Matthew didn't know what the fourth floor would look like without Sidney climbing the stairs once a week to check on him or sweeping and vacuuming the sawdust and cleaning his tools long after he'd passed out at night, for that matter. A year ago, Sidney would not have been so considerate. Matthew suspected that all the fights were Sidney's version of growing pains. After all, she was finally becoming a true adult. And when he heard them yelling in the distance he sucked in a breath, said a little prayer, and went on with his chores.

It wasn't just Sidney and Sam causing change in the store. Abigail's health was affecting his daily routines as well. She was spending more and more time at the Bookshop Hotel. Instead of letting her go straight home after her day at the bakery, AJ or Ivy would go fetch her and bring her to the hotel until the storefront closed, just like she had in the old days when Jack was running the place, as she liked to remind him. She would spend hours browsing shelves or sitting quietly in the garden, waiting for Sam's niece, Hannah, to come collect recipes. Then Matthew would come get her for dinner.

"Abigail." Matthew had a soothing voice. Abigail was grateful AJ had found him. After becoming a widow so young, many women get bitter and stoic. Abigail had feared AJ would go the way of her grandmother, Maude, and be alone forever after losing her spouse as a very young woman. But then Matthew came along, and he was such a lovely young gentleman. "Abigail, I made your favorite brisket."

She smiled at him as he offered his arm. "I thought I smelled something nice drifting in from out there."

Matthew had set up an outdoor grilling station in an area outside the garden where the lean-to had been years ago. If you stepped outside the servant's entrance by the kitchen, it was a short jaunt down the stone path there. Abigail loved that he cooked and, in fact, adored his cooking. His brisket was her favorite, and Sam always brought over potato salad and other little odds and ends. With Abigail's cupcakes and Danishes for dessert every evening, it was a wonder they weren't all enormously fat.

As she took his arm and they headed through the atrium to join the others in the café, a book slipped from Matthew's pocket.

"What is that?" she asked.

"Oh." He picked it up. "*The Heart is a Lonely Hunter.* Ivy's book club is reading it this month. You read it?"

"Hmm?" she managed as her eyes glazed softly. Something began to prod at her mind. She thought she answered the question, but perhaps she didn't. There was that thought again—the trees, a book . . . a red suit, a boy . . . her Jack . . .

Abigail

Abigail found herself looking at Jack Walters perched on a stump, reading *The Heart is a Lonely Hunter.* He was in a red bellhop uniform, his shirt pressed and tightly tucked into his pants. Sawdust and wood chips clung to his trousers.

"Whatcha reading?" Abigail asked, even though she saw the title plain as day. All the kids at school were talking about Carson McCullers because their big brothers and sisters said it was marvelous. Even Evie, who rarely cared to read, could be found with a copy tucked neatly in her pocket book. She'd spent a whole two dollars and fifty cents on that thing, two weeks' worth of her share of the laundry money.

If you asked Evelyn Lacey what was so grand about Carson Mc-Cullers, she would take a drag of her cigarette, blow smoke coolly in the air, and say, "She's twenty-two. For once, an old hag didn't write what everyone is calling great literature."

For whatever reason, Evie's style and mannerisms were straight out of the twenties. She was a girl out of her time, always wearing slinky, figureless dresses with knotted pearls when everyone else was in knee-length skirts, shirts with collars, and jackets. When her friends wore hats, Evie laid peacock feathers in her hair. She had a hang-up on *The Great Gatsby* and had considered herself Daisy Buchanan for as long as Abigail could remember. It amazed Abigail that, though she never saw Evelyn read, Evie always seemed to have a devotion to some literary character or another. Abigail imagined it was for Jack's sake. Everything was for Jack.

But Abigail didn't particularly care what Evie thought about the book. She wanted to hear Jack's thoughts.

"Hey, Abs," he said without looking up.

Abigail was nine at the time and had sneaked her older sister's copy to read when Evelyn wasn't looking. She only read it because she knew Jack would read it, even though Evie was the one who smoked and imagined herself as cool as the main character, Mick. Of the two sisters, Abigail was probably more like the tomboy than Evie. Abigail was always running around barefoot and in mud-stained clothes, looking for bugs and climbing trees.

Evelyn Lacey just liked to imagine herself as something, and she probably would be something. She had to. She was the survivor. Evelyn had been one half of a set of twins. On June 20th 1927, John and Gemma Lacey were the proud parents of two newborn daughters, Evelyn and Esme Lacey. The two new babies were bedded down together in the bassinet, and by morning, Gemma Lacey was holding a dead Esme, supposedly too small to survive the night. Evelyn was left behind with the living, wailing away with the strength of lungs that only she could have.

As a child, Abigail often speculated that when Esme had died, Evelyn had absorbed the soul of her twin into her own being. What else is a nine-year-old to think of an inexplicably cruel and often moody older sibling? Evelyn was prone to Jekyll- and Hyde-worthy mood swings, and it was some such fit that had sent Abigail running to find Jack in the middle of the afternoon. She'd run all the way to the hotel from Carson Avenue. She hadn't slowed down until she'd come to the Green, a patch of grass in the middle of the circle drive in front of the hotel.

It was a nice, warm day. Abigail's white cotton dress was covered in bits of weeds and thorns from running through an open meadow on Rose of Sharon Blvd. where no houses were built just yet. As she made her way around the covered porch of the hotel to the side servants' entrance by the kitchen, there was Jack perched on that block of wood.

He looked handsome in his red uniform, a chunk of hair flopped over one eye. He was the handsomest boy Abigail thought could ever exist. And he was Evelyn's boyfriend. Evelyn had stolen him away from his previous girlfriend, Daisy Carson, with one bat of her long eyelashes.

Abigail sat in the grass and plucked daisies a few minutes before he said anything. Then she asked him about the book.

Unlike Evelyn, he had something real to say. He talked about themes and motifs and economics and the real world and then said, "Well, Evie has read it, I think. Didn't she tell you it was marvelous?"

"Evie thinks everything is marvelous," Abigail said. She was grumpy and didn't want to talk about her sister. Her arm was sore, and her skin was starting to bruise to a nice fig color where Evelyn had pinched her just a half hour before.

"I suppose she does." Jack grinned as though this attribute were Evelyn's greatest quality. He realized his mistake and stood slightly to tuck his book in his back pocket where it didn't really fit. "Oh, Abby, come here."

The little girl hefted herself up and plopped by the stump, and Jack leaned over to rest his hand on her head. He was fourteen, the same age as Mick in the story he was reading, and his hands were slightly larger than the rest of him. They'd sat in that attitude for a few long minutes before Jack had given her head a double pat and then headed into the servants' entrance by way of the lean-to.

The lean-to was gone now. Years ago, it had been pushed back and a laundry room built in its place. Then, when AJ restored the hotel into a bookstore, she had extended the gardens and taken the lean-to out altogether. Now, sitting quietly on a garden bench, Abigail saw the place for what it was and what it had been.

Evie would have said it was marvelous.

The brisket smelled marvelous.

Matthew held her arm and asked gently, "Abigail, are you ready for dinner?"

"Oh, yes."

At the café's largest table, Matthew settled Abigail into her seat. She rather enjoyed the large dinners with AJ, Matthew, and Ivy. Even Sam came with Evie. No, not Evie. Evie was gone. It was Maude's girl, Sidney. There was something about Sidney that was so like Evie, but Abigail couldn't quite put her finger on it. Abigail suddenly realized that she'd mistaken Sidney for her dead sister and felt a knot tighten in her stomach.

At the end of dinner, Sam's niece, Hannah, came in with a tray of tarts.

"Did I get them right?" Hannah asked. She was Abigail's new baking apprentice and served Abigail the first tart, then sat down next to her.

"Almost. Your pinch of salt is too big. Make smaller pinches." With her mangled, arthritic fingers, Abigail emphatically thumped the notebook that Hannah had laid across her lap.

Hannah noticed the old woman pick her hand off the paper and move to her arm. She sat rubbing a piece of flesh on her triceps while she repeated, "Smaller pinches," again under her breath.

"Good day or bad?" AJ whispered to Matthew.

"Kind of in the middle," he said.

AJ nodded with understanding.

"What's bugging you?" Sidney asked AJ after Matthew had escorted Abigail home for the evening.

"Abigail," AJ said.

"I've been checking on her and bringing her over like you asked," Sidney said.

"I know, but it's not enough. I don't want her alone in that house every night. She needs to move in with Maude. They'd be good for each other. They could take care of each other."

"That's all well and good, AJ," Matthew said, "but what do Maude and Abigail say?"

"Abby won't have it. Maude, well, I haven't exactly asked her."

Sidney

Sidney went to Abigail's Bakery the next day. She wanted to do more, to be more useful, to be there for AJ. If AJ was worried about Abigail, then Sidney would help ease that worry. Having walked across Main Street from Aspen Court, though, she stood motionless in front of the bakery just steps away from the deli.

A sudden urge to abandon her mission and visit Sam instead came over her. Sam was just a few steps away, and the desire to be near him was overwhelming. Just thinking of seeing him made the hair on the back of her neck rise—in a good way. She could already feel his beard against the back of her neck and his hand on her hip as he hugged her good morning. He'd pour her coffee, even though she'd already had the good stuff Matthew brewed at the hotel.

She stood on the sidewalk, frozen in doubt. Sam would appreciate her visit, she justified. But Sam was a good person, so he would also understand her checking on Abigail. What no one would understand was why she was standing there, feet like concrete, unable to move on the sidewalk. Why she wanted to visit Abigail was being derailed by her addiction to Sam. Now it was too late. If she went to Sam's, she wouldn't feel good anymore. She'd feel guilty for not going to Abigail's. Her guilt would evolve into a bad mood. She'd snap at him now and pick a fight to punish herself for being so selfish and to punish him for making her selfish.

If she went to Abigail's now, she'd spend the whole time thinking about Sam and then feel ashamed. It would do Abigail no good. Sidney wasn't really much good to anyone.

Marla stepped out of Sam's. "What are you doing here?" she demanded. "No one needs you here."

I know that already, Sidney thought, but she held her chin up and looked Mrs. Finney in the eye defiantly. "I don't particularly care what you think."

"You stay away from my son," Marla said, wagging her finger in Sidney's face.

Sidney restrained herself from biting it. Shaking a finger that close to her nose as though she were a child made Sidney want to act like a child. The hag would deserve having her finger chomped on.

In the old days, she would have done it. Jude had always liked her unruliness. Most men she'd dated had enjoyed her "spunk," as they usually called it. The first time they were alone, Jude recounted how she'd put a smile on his face because he'd witnessed her telling off a teacher who'd caught her smoking on campus. He said he'd watched the fire in her eyes and thought she'd never looked prettier. She had inspired him to do something exciting and rash.

Funny how everything she was and had ever been regarding Jude was what Mrs. Finney hated. Mrs. Finney hated defiance. She hated any opinion that differed from her own. She hated free spirits. She hated teen mothers. Jude had been attracted to Sidney's defiance. He'd been intrigued by the fact that all her views were so different from those taught in his family's church. He'd made her a teen mother.

If there had never been a Jude, maybe Mrs. Finney would have been a doting mother-in-law by now. Yet if there had never been a Jude, would Sam be the kind of man Sidney even wanted?

What the hell? Where did all this self-reflection and self-doubt come from? She missed the certainty of the impulsiveness of her former lifestyle. But where had that gotten her? Here, of course.

Abigail popped her head out of her shop. "Sidney!"

Sidney was startled.

"Well, are you going to come in and help or stand out there talking to the air all day?"

By the look of Mrs. Finney's face, she was startled, too.

Sidney supposed Abigail couldn't see Marla under the stoop, standing a little behind one of the shopping center's signs. She was relieved to be saved, but confused that Abigail had presumed Sidney was there for her all along. Sidney hadn't told anyone she was coming.

Sidney didn't speak to or look at Marla. She just walked into the bakery and let out a deep sigh. "I was just talking to Mrs. Finney," she explained.

Abigail let the door close. "Oh, I know," she said. If she'd been the winking type, Sidney supposed the old woman might have winked at her just then, but Abigail stepped into the kitchen. "I have tarts burning. Hannah helps me from time to time, but I imagine she gets caught up over there."

"What do you need me to do?" Sidney asked.

A wave of confusion came over the woman. "What, Evie?"

Outside, it began to rain again.

Marla

Marla glanced up from her knitting as the thunder outside rattled the roof. It had been such a rainy year. Rain after rain. Then, just when she thought the rain would stop, it would rain some more. She shifted in her seat, readjusting her long skirt as the fat from one thigh rubbed against that of the other. It wasn't an especially warm day, and Sam was about keeping the deli cool, but she was sweaty and increasingly uncomfortable.

She used a free knitting needle to reach behind her and scratch an itch on her back and was caught in that awkward position when her stepdaughter's girl, Hannah, came into the store.

"Where's Uncle Sam?"

"Across the way." It seemed he was always "across the way" these days. Always running sandwiches to the café inside the Bookshop Hotel, always taking breaks from his own work to see that Sidney or do something for her illegitimate daughter. Everyone liked to forget that fact, for some reason—that AJ was fatherless. Marla didn't forget.

"Ah."

Marla eyed Hannah as she put on an apron and got to work in the deli. Hannah looked so much like Sam's father, so much how she'd imagined their own little girls looking—so much how Hannah's mother had looked.

"Who's this?" Marla remembered asking just weeks after their wedding.

The girl was lounging in the living room reading a book while Marla's new husband, Frank, leaned back in his recliner drinking a beer. She was plump in a childish sort of way and had bits of strawberry in her hair and a few freckles. The strawberry would later turn to a dark blonde, and the freckles disappear with age, but still later, when the girl grew up and had her own children, that look would return to Marla's house in the form of so-called grandchildren—grandchildren who weren't really hers.

"My kid, Christy," he said with a shrug. As though it were nothing to have an illegitimate daughter lurking about the town and now in their home. "Nothing to worry about. Her mother is married. Kid just wanted to meet her real dad."

"Biological, not real," the girl corrected him. She had a critical eye that was not genetically her own. It looked like one she had learned and now mimicked. Her natural features lent themselves to laziness, like Finn.

That was all the information Marla was offered. After Frank Finney left and everyone was sure he wouldn't be coming back, Connie came to Marla and proposed a peace. "Let them be siblings," she said. "Christy would love to be in his life." By that time, the girl was so much older than Sam, there wasn't much to do except let them enjoy a few holidays together here and there. Marla supposed there wouldn't be much harm in that and acquiesced.

Sam, however, took to having a sister immediately, and he was nothing but the perfect little brother ever since. From the moment he found out, he insisted on visiting every week. As he got older, he joined Connie's family for dinner as often as he could.

When Christy married and had her own family, Sam continued to have dinner with her family once a week and gave her kids jobs at the deli shop when they were old enough to work. Christy had a lot of kids, and most of them worked the register for Sam at some point in time or another, but Hannah and Sam got along the best, and she was the only one who kept coming back. Hannah was determined to take over the deli one day, and Sam was happy to plan for it.

Marla remained civil to everyone for Sam's sake, but she didn't like it, and she let everyone know she didn't like it. All of her attempts at civility felt insincere. She didn't like Hannah marching around acting like she owned the place. Hannah might be Sam's blood, but it irked Marla to no end that the girl wasn't her own.

Instead, she was the blood of that tramp Finn, the worst human being Marla could fathom. The man who swept her off her feet, parading around with a cute nickname like Finn, married her, gave her a son, then walked out her back door and never came back. Frank Finney, who got to run around having babies that he never took care of. How unfair that the little girl she'd dreamed of having one day was someone else's.

Marla didn't know the full details of Hannah's mother's birth, but she did know that Finn had been young. He had to have been. She also knew that Connie had to have been old enough to get married the same year and cover up the scandal sufficiently. So when that little babysitter, Sidney, showed up pregnant, Marla felt certain she'd seduced her own little man. Never mind that being the most unlikely and illogical conclusion. No one seemed to be sure who the father was, and that justified Marla's feelings on the matter. What was Marla to think when she knew her son to be smitten with the girl?

Now Hannah turned on the oven to get started on a melt for a customer, and Marla shifted again in her seat. "Must you, Hannah? It's so warm." Then she looked up and saw it was for Mrs. Carson, Jude's mother, who was rolling her eyes.

"Don't bother toasting or melting anything," she said, waving her hand. "I'll eat it cold."

Hannah turned the oven off and handed the sandwich on a plate to Mrs. Carson.

"It's early to be eating sandwiches." Marla looked at the clock. Sam still wasn't back from his seven o'clock delivery to the Hotel. The rain was coming down pretty heavily, so she imagined he was loitering in the hotel with the tramp.

"I didn't really come to eat," she said, sitting down at the café table with Marla. Marla's legs tingled from the pressure of sitting for too long. "I want to talk about this wedding."

"What's it to you?"

"Sidney is my granddaughter's mother."

"And?"

Mrs. Carson didn't seem to know what to say after that.

"Let me ask you something, Barbara. Have you ever been to any of AJ's birthday parties?"

"No."

"Did you attend her wedding?"

Mrs. Carson didn't respond. She had attended, against the advice of her husband, but she'd stood far in the back and hadn't signed the guest book. As far as she knew, no one except AJ knew she'd been there.

"Did you see her graduate college or go to her husband's funeral?" Marla pressed.

"No." Mrs. Carson felt ashamed. The whole town had been at Kevin Rhys' funeral, and again, her husband had advised that she stay home and busy herself. Reverend Carson, her father-in-law, had not been pleased with his son. It wasn't a very good move politically, either.

"You're not family," Marla said. "You have no business worrying about her mother or my son."

"I just thought I could help . . . make it special."

"Not happening. She doesn't deserve special. My son is not marrying that girl, and he certainly doesn't need or want your involvement."

Barbara Carson's eyes grew wide. "I didn't realize."

"You didn't ask."

Marla had attended AJ's wedding. She'd sewn elaborate tablecloths for the girl's reception. It hadn't been for AJ; it had been for Sam. Sam had catered the wedding, and Marla wanted his hard work to be properly presented. Everyone needed to remember Sam's food. After all, her son was worth remembering. Her son was important. These other people were a lot of tramps and liars. She simultaneously hated them and wanted their approval.

It had taken months to sew those tablecloths. Marla didn't have natural skill, but she'd needed work after Sam's father abandoned them, and she had become the home economics teacher at the school. She had forced herself to learn things that had always interested her anyway, and she'd practiced a lot.

It had been easy to feel motivated to learn to sew and crochet, as she'd already been working hard at knitting for years. She'd used her mistakes as teaching tools for her students, covering the embarrassment of messing up in front of them with long lectures and words of wisdom. When Sam had first opened the deli, she'd had him come in as a special guest speaker to teach the kids a few basic cooking techniques.

She might not have wanted to be at Sidney's daughter's wedding, but she was, and she was proud of her son. She handed sandwiches to people as they came near the tables. She spied Sidney there and gave her a dirty look or two. After the ceremony and fifteen minutes into the reception, she grew weary. Her ankles were swollen, and her limbs ached from standing. She kissed her son on the cheek and went home. She went to bed early, exhausted from the event.

The next morning, Marla searched the house for her boy. "Sammy, Sam." He was a grown man, of course, but he'd always be her boy. Her baby boy.

Sam wasn't home. It was seven in the morning. She was already in the kitchen by the time it dawned on her that the house was empty. She prepared waffle mix and poured it into the iron before plodding back to his room to check the still-made bed again.

Marla hovered in the doorway of the empty room, a broken, abandoned woman. First her husband, now her son.

See, Finn hadn't left her suddenly, not really. He'd left in little steps over time. The first argument after their marriage, he had rolled his eyes and said, "We should never have married." Little, quiet mutterings, frustrations, louder temper tantrums, and one huge argument later, he'd asked for a divorce. She had refused to give it to him. She'd cried and convinced him to stay.

That's when the drinking had begun.

Marla lived a life knowing those closest to her always had one foot out the door. Every disagreement with Finn had resulted in a threat to leave, which had turned to weekend fishing trips that had grown longer and longer. Finally, he'd just stayed away. Of course, she'd cried. But part of her had been relieved. There was no balance to maintain, no explosion to anticipate.

For so long, Marla had lived crippled by the thought that no matter what decision she made, it was the wrong one. Pork roast for dinner and he'd complain that it was too bland; chicken was too spicy. Choose not to cook at all and he'd call her lazy. Forget making traditional staples like spaghetti or meat loaf—none of it lived up to his mother's. After a week of unsatisfactory dinners, divorce had been his favorite topic of discussion. It had been an endless once-a-week cycle.

By the time Finn forgot to come home, Marla had been worn out. Money for groceries would be an issue. Her mind had reeled at the practicality of how to live without Finn, how to raise a child without a man.

Then she'd looked at her boy and known she'd figure it out. She'd looked at her boy and known she at least had one man, no matter how small and helpless, who would love her forever. Little boys, she knew from her own husband, loved their mothers unconditionally and were oblivious to their faults. Sam, by sheer virtue of being her son—her child—would adore her cooking no matter how bland or spicy. It was how she kept house that would become his standard for life. How she dressed would be how he expected respectable women to dress. It was the nature of boys to worship their mothers.

But today, years later, he was missing. He hadn't come home or slept in his own bed last night. She knew he was at that tramp's daughter's wedding yesterday. Marla's fist went to her mouth, though no one was there to see her gasp. Her son had spent the night with a woman, and not just any woman—that girl. That slut.

The waffle iron beeped, and Marla went to pull them out, but she heard the back door creak open.

"Hey, Mama." Sam was sheepish under her glare.

"Sam."

"Breakfast?" His curls splayed across his forehead. His suit coat was over his arm, and his shirt from the day before was wrinkled.

Marla pulled the waffles out with a fork and tossed them on a plate. Sam didn't even bother to butter or syrup them. He ate them silently, even though they were burnt, and Marla could see that he didn't like the way they tasted. She winced, waiting for a derogatory comment that would never come out of the mouth of her son. She still always expected one.

He polished off the food, got a glass of milk, and finished it in one gulp. He kissed her cheek and said, "Thank you, Mama. I love you." Then he left the room.

Marla sat down at the table and hardened herself against the tears she felt welling up behind her eyes.

Sidney

Sam was principled in a way that Sidney could never quite understand. Loyalty was what got him every time. He was loyal to Lily Hollow, loyal to his mother, and loyal to his sister and their entire clan, despite the tension it obviously created. To make things easy, Sidney would have just picked one side and dropped the other.

But Sam wanted everyone happy. Sam wanted to die knowing he had done everything as right as he possibly could. How many times had she heard him say he "wanted to do right by" some person or another. That was why everyone liked Sam but no one was very close to him. You can't trust the mediator one hundred percent all the time. They won't pick you—they'll ride the fence. At least that's how Sidney saw it. Sam was always riding the fence.

That wasn't entirely fair. She backpedaled against her own mind. Sam had explained himself before, and when he said it, it sounded sweet and good. When he said it, it sounded so damn righteous, it rendered Sidney speechless. Sam believed that his decisions had to stand on their own. If you were to make a list, one line at a time, of all you had ever done in life, would your actions speak for themselves? Or would you have some explaining to do?

Never talking to his mother again would always be out of the question. What kind of person never talks to their mother again?

Someone with a cranky mother. Done and done in Sidney's world. She thought back to the years of silence between her and Maude. Had that made her feel better? A little, sometimes. Did that make it right? Not by Sam's standards.

To be fair to Sam, he also didn't obey every one of Mrs. Finney's whims. She didn't want him to be friends with Mr. Finney's other daughter. She'd been pretty irritable about him demanding to be a brother. Even though they were all family now, the woman was still obviously cranky about spending time with them and nearly hostile toward Hannah when she worked at the deli.

"See there?" Sam said to Sidney once. "Mama justifies being mean real well. But how can being mean to someone because of who their daddy is be worth explanation?"

"Can't we be mean because she's mean?" Sidney argued. "That seems pretty valid."

"Nope. It's still saying that you're mean."

"You're mean to me all the time."

"Mean and stern aren't the same thing." And with that, the man kissed her forehead and completely infuriated her by calming her. She hated that he always proved himself right and comforted her at the end of every discussion. It made her angry, being so wholly wrong all the time.

And there lay the problem. *In every relationship, except AJ and Matthew's*, Sidney thought bitterly, *there's a good person and a bad person.* Sidney hadn't been the good person since Jude, and look where that had gotten her. Everyone thought she was the hussy that had seduced the preacher's perfect grandson. Being the bad person is all well and good on short-lived flings around the globe.

But not now. Not with the person you wanted to grow old with. How utterly frustrating it would be to always be the jerk, the grinch, the one with the bad ideas. But being the good one sounded boring and also nerve-wracking to be tied to someone with such flawed values. Poor Sam. He must hate her!

Sidney took a drag off her cigarette and vowed for the thousandth time that it would be her last. Sam hated that she smoked. He didn't care for women who smelled like ashtrays. Yet here he was professing to love her, a smoker.

Was she selfish to keep smoking? Probably. To be fair on herself, it was far less when she was around Sam. She could go hours—whole days—without smoking if she wanted to, as long as he didn't bring up his mother. Mrs. Finney could have her chain smoking in two minutes flat.

"Sidney." Matthew rapped his knuckles on her door.

"Shit." She fumbled with the cigarette like a caught teenager, and it burned her hand.

"Sidney, you can't smoke in here. You'll damage the books." She smashed it and flicked the butt out the window, ran to the work table in the middle processing room, and poured lighter fluid all over the sticker on Maeve Binchy's *Nights of Rain and Stars*. The smell did little to hide the cigarette smoke, but the previous store's sticker started peeling right off the book without damaging the jacket.

"Sidney, unlock the door."

"Oh, is it locked?" She popped up and opened the door for Matthew who was standing there with one arm raised to bang again while the other was overflowing with books.

"Smoking cigarettes in a room of paper drenched in lighter fluid? Sidney. Use your brain." She was indignant for a second. Her daughter's boyfriend, at least fifteen years her junior, talking to her like that! Then again, you can't argue with that logic. What was she thinking? It dawned on her how awful their entire situation could have been. Not just the smell of smoke in AJ's inventory, but she could have very well lit them all on fire. Matthew could not have been more polite about it.

She opened the window again to let the room air out and sat back down to her chore for the day, cleaning and pricing these books while AJ made gala arrangements. The white "$8.17, item #383101," peeled off with ease under the tool in Sidney's hand. The lighter fluid dried and showed that it had done no damage to the picture of the girl on the cover. She wiped away the remaining residue with a paper towel, and the trade-sized paperback looked brand new again. Sidney peeked at the inside and read the first line.

AJ appeared in the doorway, and Sidney felt ashamed for being caught reading instead of working when AJ had been working so hard to put this event together and all she needed was a little inside help.

"Have you read this one?" Sidney asked meekly.

"No. But I'll read it with you some time."

Sidney nodded, priced it at $7, and moved on to cleaning the next book on the stack: T.C. Boyle's *The Tortilla Curtain*. AJ grabbed some papers off a table near the door and disappeared as quietly as she had come.

Later, Sidney had her chin propped on her knuckles, staring into the space between her and the door of the hotel. Ivy blocked her gaze when she came barging through the door, all legs and dreadlocks.

"You could shoot lasers out of those eyes, looks like," Ivy said and glanced behind her out into the world. "You trying to hit Sam from the register? You'd have to have some serious aim."

"No, I'm not mad at Sam." She was mad at her own imperfections. She was mad that she'd gotten caught smoking in the workroom. More than that, she was mad at herself for having been smoking in there in the first place. She knew that someone would say something, and then Sam would find out that she'd been caught smoking in the workroom and be disappointed in her. He'd never do something so reckless. So she was a little mad. She was mad at Sam for never struggling to do what was right; doing right always seemed to come to him naturally.

"Could have fooled me." Ivy shrugged and disappeared upstairs.

Not really mad. No, Sidney corrected herself. Flustered was the word. She was just flustered. She remembered a time when he'd said she was perfect. So simply, "You're perfect." The words came like a cat's purr. Almost breathless, but at the same time, heavy.

Little Sammy-Finns had grown into this man who could completely melt her down to barest desires, and it was comforting and wonderful and terrifying.

She had run from the hotel that morning after AJ's wedding.

She'd waited until he passed out, nuzzled into her stomach. The beginning of beard stubble scratched against her skin, and she liked it, already regretting her decision to walk out that door as soon as his breathing settled.

Just as she made a move to get up, his oversized arm flung around her and wedged itself around her hip, between her bone and the sheets. Oh God, he was the most comfortable man alive. She wanted nothing more than to burrow down into his arms and the mattress and stay there forever. But she couldn't. She wouldn't.

Once out from under his hand, she debated leaving him a note on the Hotel pad. "Sorry, Sam"? No, "Sammy-Finns – I . . ."? No. There was nothing she could say. This was doomed from the start. Doomed from the first time she'd walked into his mother's house at age twelve. Doomed from the moment Jude had claimed her life. Just doomed.

She pried open the window, lit a cigarette, and watched him sleep a moment. His curls were a mop, coming loose from the gel he had used to tame it for the wedding. His eyelids were thick and heavy, little orange lashes brushing against the freckles on his cheek.

No, she would leave.

And she did.

No wonder his mother hated her so much. She had so many imperfections, and Mrs. Finney, despite all her ill tempers, had somehow produced an amazing son. It only made sense that she would want to protect him from people like herself.

The postman interrupted her thoughts when he came through the front doors and stood under the heavy chandelier of the Bookshop Hotel's entryway.

"Deliveries," he said.

Ivy met him and signed for the packages, and he left.

After a moment of sorting through bills and a few packages most likely containing books AJ had purchased for either herself or the store, Ivy came to a single tiny box with a local stamp. It looked like a gift. "This one is for you," Ivy said.

Ivy handed it to Sidney and then sat, tapping her pen into her sketchpad, dying to see what was inside. It had the Finneys' address in the return label as clear as day. She loved living through Sidney's torrid romance and couldn't wait to discover what little gift the man had purchased for his girlfriend this time.

Marla Finney kept a horde of things no one would ever want or care about. Where most people saw a pile of junk in the garage or hall closet, Marla saw an infinite number of treasures, memories, or potential memories. Like a raccoon or a magpie, she liked shiny objects. Brass really got her excited, as it was shiny and inexpensive, so she could collect it in abundance.

Sam could never quite wrap his head around this trait of his mother's, but he went with it, knowing it was at its worst on days she was thinking about his dad, or rather the lack of his dad.

It was in the nature of both mother and son to be gift givers. Marla loved sharing her piles of treasure troves, knick-knacks, and handmade items with everyone she knew—or with everyone still in her good graces since the last holiday. Marla had quite the habit of feeling snubbed. Sam, on the other hand, had acquired some mysterious calm that allowed for most anything to roll off his shoulders. Though the people he referred to as "friends" were few, there was never any doubt as to who those people were.

Sidney knew this about the family she found herself desperately longing to join, and as she thought about Sam's perpetual gift giving, she felt a goofy smile plaster across her face and tried to remind herself not to gape like a fool. She loved presents. She really loved expensive presents, and she'd gotten presents from Sam before. One thing that man knew how to do was win a girl over with a gift, especially if he'd thought she'd been throwing darts at him with her eyes, which apparently everyone thought she did often.

Ivy flipped the card open. "It says his mother sends her regards."

"Yeah, that means she hates me right now."

"No, it's actually from his mother, and she sends her regards," Ivy said again.

Sidney tore open the box and found a little scrap of paper inside. "Gone fishing."

"What does that mean?" Ivy asked.

"Nothing. It's just Mrs. Finney being Mrs. Finney."

"Who went fishing?"

"Sam's dad. About thirty years ago."

Sam

"I'm sorry. I didn't know she was going to send that. I didn't think . . ."

"You just didn't think, Sam. Of course she'd send something like that. She hates me."

"Well, you're kind of . . ."

"What? What am I? Hate-able?"

"Sometimes! Yes. You are hate-able!"

She was fuming. She was too tired to fume at him anymore, and he could see that. Instead of continuing the fight, she just walked off. Immediately, he was sorry, but he didn't want to yell that after her.

He turned and headed home, knowing she'd come to him when she was good and ready and not until then.

Sam sat on the porch at his mother's house, surveying the street. The sun was setting low, and he'd closed the deli a mere half hour before. His curls still dripped from his shower, and his white T-shirt clung to him where he hadn't completely dried off properly.

It had been a year or so since Sidney had come back to Lily Hollow to live with AJ. Sam didn't quite keep track of the time well. There was life with Sidney and life without, and life without Sidney was best left in the back of his mind. But damn, life with Sidney was a roller coaster ride at best. The woman got under his skin like no one else. And he loved her like no one else.

They'd had a fight again. It was typical, them fighting these days. Get married, don't get married. Go travel, don't go travel. His mother, his mother, his mother. Things came back to his mother a lot. He knew his mom had hurt Sidney very badly when they were younger. She'd cut Sidney off, quit letting her babysit, and said horrible things about her at the church. A high school kid didn't deserve that, even if she had gotten pregnant.

Marla Finney had not been kind to Sidney Montgomery, but Marla Finney wasn't generally known as an overtly kind woman, so Sam hadn't really thought much of it until it became the issue of every discussion and every argument with the woman he was bound and determined to spend the rest of his life with.

Garrick Brighton whizzed by in his daddy's new truck, and Sam hollered at him to slow down. "Could have run over the turtle," he muttered. He stood up and walked the stretch of yard to the street. Hardly anyone came through this time of day, and when they did, most people crept through the roads of Lily Hollow at a snail's pace. In high school, they used to race up and down Swan Lane, but as of late, kids weren't even really doing that anymore. They were too busy playing on their smart phones. Despite all that, he was on a turtle rescue mission, because someone had almost squashed one.

The turtle had made it to the yellow stripe in the road and was hunkered down in hiding. When Sam scooped it up, he expected its head to duck farther into his shell. Instead, it did the exact opposite. The little guy peered out at him. The two looked at each other, reptile and man sizing each other up.

"I'll get you someplace safe," he said and headed to the side yard. Sam poked around a bit in the calla lily garden and tucked the turtle under the shade of one of the taller plants. Standing back, he was unsatisfied and found a few items in the shed to prop into the dirt.

"Building him a house?" Sidney asked.

"Sneaking up on people in the dark?"

"It's what I'm good at."

He ignored her and kept fiddling with his makeshift turtle structure.

"You don't have to do that, you know. His house is on his back. He can take care of himself."

As though he hadn't heard the last bit, he said, "You're good at sneaking away in the dark, too. In fact, you've made quite a habit of it."

She shrugged as he abandoned the turtle to turn around and look Sidney square in the face. Sam looked at her the same way he'd looked at her a hundred times before, asking the same question. She leaned toward him and whispered, "I don't trust your mom to actually be as long as she says she will."

They made their way back to the porch, where he sat in his chair and she crawled into his lap, resting her head on his chest. They listened to Lily Hollow wind down into sleep.

"I want to buy Abigail's house," he said, breaking the silence.

"Abigail's? Why Abigail's?" She yawned.

Sam closed his eyes, summoning his patience. "Because she's old. AJ has been trying to get her to move in with Maude so someone will be around to help her. And I need a house. We all win."

Sidney's breathing fell into rhythm with the thudding of his heartbeat, and she didn't answer.

"I want my own place," he continued. "I do. I think this is a good solution that will be nice for everyone."

He looked down at her head. Her hair scooped to the side made her look barely older than when he'd first met her. The darkness shielded his eyes from her smile lines and the sun damage from French beaches. Right here, right now, she looked like a teenager again. She looked like the Sidney he'd first fallen in love with. He wrapped his big arms around her as she drifted into sleep and mumbled something about a house being nice.

He looked back to the yard and noticed a glint in the moonlight. He squinted a bit and saw that it was the turtle from the garden making its way ever so slowly to the end of the yard. He shook his head at it.

"By morning, you'll be road kill," he said to the turtle. The turtle stopped as though it understood, and it turned to face him. "I saved you. I made you a house. It would be nice if you appreciated it."

The turtle continued its crawl to the street.

George

George Edelstein, Jr. eyed his overlong beard in the mirror. He was beginning to look like his father, and just thinking that caused his bushy eyebrows to furrow. He took the trimmers out and trimmed the beard back short, then slowly and carefully took an old-fashioned razor to his face. His father's old razor kit.

It was nostalgia and grief, really, because George had never much cared for anything of his father's, anything old, anything that reminded him of hoarding and collecting and saving. Instead, he liked new things. He liked technology, the latest gadget, the latest everything. When he got a new thing, he got rid of the old.

Not Dad. Dad had taken great pains to care for every object he'd ever beheld, and most of his objects had been books. Great books, expensive books, old books, rare books, books that had simply struck his fancy in some way. The more contemporary titles had been toted to book signings and been graced with the pen of the author so that they had some reason for being housed next to their antiquarian counterparts. George had always been annoyed with Dad's obsessions: the books, the butterflies, all the collections that could put a museum to shame.

Chin smooth now, he peered into the mirror again. His father's face was gone, and he sighed. He'd spent a few too many months trying to decide how he felt about everything—all of it—and today, he had a meeting with a lawyer. Apparently, some bookstore had bought Dad's collection. His dad's collection. A collection that should go from father to son, as Dad had always said. He had been too proud to take it then. He didn't want it and had told his father so when the man lay dying of prostate cancer in a hospital bed.

But now, now that it was being packed up and shipped to a bookstore—now that it would be out of his life forever—he wanted it. He saw the treasures, he saw his dad's face light up over a particular title. Mostly, he saw a massive, empty library in a house that was now his to keep. Everything about it was wrong and unsettling.

George checked his watch. It was time to go. He wanted to get to the meeting with the lawyer early, as it was his only hope in getting the library put back where it belonged. No way was he going to let his Dad's life's work be picked off one by one by people who had no business calling themselves collectors. They didn't know what it took to be a real collector. They didn't know how many hours of research and care had gone into these books. No one knew. No one knew but the Edelsteins, and therefore, the books would stay with the Edelsteins.

When George got to the coffeeshop, the lawyer was already there. He didn't like that he wasn't the first to arrive. That was unusual. He checked his watch. It was more than a half hour before their meeting was meant to begin. Of course, had he arrived first and sat and waited for his lawyer, he would have been annoyed at the lack of punctuality and forethought.

What should he do? He didn't want it to be discovered that he was a control freak who came more than thirty minutes early to appointments. The lawyer looked up and waved. Too late, he'd been spotted. George felt a little defeated and made a motion to head to the bar to order, but the lawyer made a gesture to the table and scooted a coffee across to an open chair.

"I knew you would be early," she said as he approached the table.

He felt his heavy brows furrow. She passed some papers across and tapped the table with a pen. "The firm told me to be early," she said.

"Ah."

"Family trait?"

"I suppose," he said. Actually, it wasn't a family trait at all. His father had been late to everything, always off discovering something and forgetting about responsibilities. Things like dinner, picking his children up from their very posh private school, and divorce hearings with George's mother were beyond George, Sr.

"So, it seems your father left a list of bookstores to be contacted in the event of his death and that his collection was to be sold to the highest bidder among them and the money to be dispersed among his living children."

"Yes."

"You were not satisfied with the amount deposited in your account, of which . . ." She slipped a pair of reading glasses on and peered down at another set of papers. "You actually inherited it all?"

"No. I mean, yes. I was satisfied with the amount. I am the only living child." His brother had drunk himself to death just before his father's condition was discovered. Having an alcoholic little brother had never made it easy to be the eldest. Having a preoccupied father had never made it easy to be an Edelstein. Being the last Edelstein and still unmarried and very much alone was making it quite difficult to manage being human. "I just want to keep it. The collection. The books. I want them. I want them back in the library—in my father's library—in my house where they belong. That's all I want."

The lawyer looked up at him and leaned back in her chair. She took her reading glasses off and looked him over. She took a drink of coffee, put her glasses back on, and said, "I think I can work with that."

AJ

The first of the collection arrived by freight, and AJ gasped in excitement. They'd broken the bank bidding on this collection. The Bookshop Hotel had managed to land itself on the list of contenders—all small mom-and-pop shops like her own—and she was beside herself with excitement. Tales of the great bibliophile George Edelstein, Sr. had been floating around the book world long before she'd ever become a bookstore owner, and she'd often dreamed of visiting his library.

Now, in the workroom, she sat with boxes of antiquarian and rare collectibles with more pride than seemed reasonable. These books were hers! People all around the world would give an arm or a leg for some of these titles. Well, some people—her kind of people. Of course, they were going to have to be sold. She couldn't keep them for herself forever, but for now, she got to touch them. Ivy would be taking digital photos of each, so they'd at least be able to keep the memories of them, too.

She unpacked the first box and basked in the glory of just the first title. It was *Don Quixote*, illustrated by Ricardo Balaca in 1880. So beautiful. Worth thousands.

She wondered how many others like this were in the collection. If there were more gemstones like this, the Bookshop Hotel wouldn't have to worry about being in the red for years to come.

A knock came on the door, interrupting her wonder.

"AJ." It was Matthew's nervous voice. She didn't hear that from him often. "AJ, bad news."

He walked in and handed her a letter. "Just came by certified mail."

It was from George Edelstein, Jr.'s lawyer, contesting the sale of the books. Contesting her right to own them, to keep them, to sell them. She stared at the letter, not in shock, and not even in calm surrender. She knew it had all been too good to be true. She knew the rug would get ripped from under her gently curling toes sooner or later. Hadn't it all been too easy? Hadn't she been waiting for reality to set in?

She let her hand rest on the book and tapped the letter against her forehead with the other. "Of course," was all she could say in response.

Matthew

Of course? That was it? No fight? No questions? He had a million. How didn't she? Was she giving up? He eyed her with suspicion. For all that Sidney was over the top, AJ could be annoyingly calm. At first, the calm had been soothing to him, so different from what he was used to. But sometimes, her lack of reaction *was* her big reaction. She buried frustrations and worked them out on her own. Got caught up in her head and sometimes forgot to lean on him.

She shut him out. She shut everyone out.

In that way, she had gotten something from Sidney. Where Sidney chose to run away from her problems, AJ stayed put but locked herself away from them, shielding herself.

Her "of course" sounded like nails on a chalkboard to him. He could already see her thinking through the problem, eager to push him out of the room.

He wanted her to open up to him, to admit there was trouble and she didn't know how to fix it, ask his advice, work it out together. She wouldn't do that. She'd work it out in her head first and then lay out the plan to him as an order. She would be polite, but it would be an order nonetheless.

He didn't like to fight, and really, there was nothing to fight about, so he said nothing and just waited in the doorway. She looked at him, puzzled, and he had every opportunity to express himself but didn't want to stress her out. She didn't need this, Sam and Sidney with their explosive relationship and her safe haven being attacked by an Edelstein.

What could Edelstein do? he wondered. Would he just keep the gala from happening, or could it get worse? How could he even stop it? What right did he have? The transaction was made between AJ and George Edelstein, Sr., so what grounds were there?

All the answers were buried in that envelope that Matt wouldn't be able to look over until AJ was done digesting it all. He should have read the whole packet and not just the top page of the letter before handing it to her. Then he would know what they were up against.

"Do you need something?" she asked.

His brow furrowed.

Sam

Sam had been looking for Sidney, but she wasn't in the rare book room working like he had presumed. It was AJ sitting there instead, with Matthew handing over bad news. They didn't speak on the topic, but Sam could feel the aura of distress from both of them and AJ's un-spoken frustration. He decided to duck out. Selfishly, he didn't want to know the details. Selfishly, he didn't care. He was looking for Sidney. He was sure to find her in some crisis or another, and he could only handle one crisis at a time.

Finding her wasn't so difficult. She was taking a nap in her room. He let himself in and stood over her a minute, trying to decide what to do. Before he decided, one eye popped open.

"Sam."

"Hey, Sid."

"What's up?"

"I just had some time to kill and thought we could go for a walk." He needed to coexist with her a few minutes without argument or drama. He just wanted to spend time with her that didn't entail life-changing decision-making.

She seemed to sense this and got out of bed. "You going to let me change into something other than yoga pants?"

He ducked out and went downstairs to wait in the café.

They'd been walking for more than an hour, not completely silent, but not really talking about much. It was a relief. Then she said something that sounded like the beginning of a nag. It sounded like the beginning of all he was trying to avoid.

"So, what are your plans for this week?"

Sure, that's casual enough, but Sidney never said something like that casually. She wanted to know if he planned to talk to his mother. If he wanted to get a house together. She was casually pressing for information, and it frustrated him.

He dropped her hand and stood back to take her in, her posture and facial expression. Sam wasn't good at picking up on things. He often misread them. He was known for assuming the best in people and dismissing people's faults. He was made aware of this attribute quite keenly when he was young, and for that reason, he didn't allow people to get real close anymore.

He lived with an oppressive mother, and lately, his best friends had been his girlfriend's daughter and her boyfriend. He discussed more with Abigail—the two business owners in the same strip had started a relationship as strong as their successful businesses—and Mr. Henry, who religiously bought coffee as soon as Sam opened the deli doors, than anyone else.

Being friendly with everyone didn't mean you had a lot of friends. And as he soaked in Sidney's presence and everything she meant to him and everything he supposed he meant to her, he found himself wondering what he had missed. What not-so-small detail about her personality was going to burn him? His mother was dismissive and ugly about everyone. He had never once valued her opinion on the matter. However, just because Mrs. Finney hated everyone didn'tmean that her dislike for Sidney was completely unwarranted. His mother's nagging entered his mind, and just for a moment, it didn't sound like nagging. It sounded like love.

Sidney took his hand just then. "No, walk me home."

He relaxed instantly, and all his previous speculations vanished. At least for the walk home.

Abigail

Another rainstorm. Abigail glanced out her own dining room window. It had long ceased to be formal and was dressed up more like a breakfast nook would be. Her mother's good china cabinet had been emptied of anything worth anything during the Depression and had since been filled with a first-edition copy of every book Sidney's grandfather, Jack Walters, had ever published. Abigail had never been much of a reader, but she did read every book Jack wrote and had tried to make time for his favorites, too.

The rain poured over the bay window, pattering in rhythm to her heartbeat and the flutter of birds' wings in the garden as they dodged the rain. She could see them flapping about in the tomatoes. The glass panes were so thin, she could hear them a bit, too. All the bedroom windows had been replaced with double-paned glass over the years. Things changed so much through time, even in houses. Energy-efficient this, storm-protection that. But the dining-room window remained exactly as it was the day her father had built the window seat into the bay and scooted the table up to it.

"With a bench there, we can fit more people at the table." On holidays, all the kids were crammed into the window seat, and Mama's family took over the grown-up chairs.

Abigail had sat in the window area for so long, she'd never stopped. She'd eaten her morning toast and eggs, alone at the table, for fifty years now. She'd never married, never left home. Everyone had passed on, and she'd been left with the house she was born in. An old house.

The rain came down more heavily, and the pane rattled. It hadn't rained so hard in years. She had a mind to go out and romp in it, but she was afraid she might slip and fall—or worse, afraid she might encounter a few ghosts.

When Abigail stood in the rain, all she could see around her was Jack Walters broken and crying in the road. It didn't matter how many years had passed, how many storms had come. It didn't matter that Jack had evolved into the great patriarch of all of Lily Hollow, that he had reached a level of quietly spoken celebrity as an author, or that he was now gone from their lives and residing in the great hereafter. It didn't matter.

Whenever it rained, all Abigail saw, felt, and smelled were the memories from that day. That moment. That Jack.

There was a rap on the porch door. "Abigail?" a familiar voice called, but Abigail couldn't place it. "Abigail, it's Sidney."

Oh, Sidney, the poor dear. Always fighting with that Sam. No one could understand why, except maybe Abigail did a little. Hearts are broken long before they're ever born. Heritage and history predetermine so much, maybe too much. Sidney would be different if Maude had been different. Maude would have been different if Jack had been better. Jack would have been better if he hadn't been in love with . . . Well, Abigail, thought, to understand Sidney you'd have to have known *her*. And no one knew *her*. Not anymore.

"AJ sent me to fetch you!" Sidney yelled from the porch. "Something about wanting you to come hang out at the Hotel today, if that's okay with you."

The Hotel. The Bookshop Hotel now. Across the street from the bakery. Oh dear. She'd forgotten to open the bakery.

AJ

Matthew had been hovering ever since he'd seen the letter about the Edelstein collection. He was expecting something from AJ, but she was too stressed out to worry about what was bothering him. The Bookshop Hotel and this gala were her priorities, and George Edelstein was threatening that.

She looked through the paperwork. She was solid. All the t's were crossed, and all the i's were dotted. Her contract, the purchase of the estate, everything—Edelstein didn't have a leg to stand on. She'd sent notarized letters, she'd met with lawyers, she'd done research, she knew she was covered. She knew the bookstore would be fine. At least it should be fine. She knew the gala would be fine. At least it should be fine as well, if the courts honored her impeccable paperwork. Still, clearly, she was nervous.

She did what she always did with nervous energy. She did more research, wrote more letters, and stayed up late preparing things for the gala. She continued to inventory books. She went over financials with the bank. And when she couldn't sleep at night, she read boring history books that might relax her nerves.

Surprisingly, Sidney—of all people—had begun to be helpful. She was alleviating some of AJ's stress by diligently processing incoming merchandise to give AJ more time to work on the Edelstein books. She had begun waking up in a timely fashion and brought AJ coffee from the café when it got too busy for Matthew to abandon his barista duties.

When AJ got wrapped up in her head and notices from lawyers, her mother knew when to leave her alone and when to chatter. Her mother knew when to take the chatter of the bookstore patrons elsewhere. Her mother knew when to occupy Ivy, and the two had actually begun to work together to find their own projects around the store. AJ found herself comforted by Sidney's presence, despite the ongoing tension and fights with Sam. A year ago, had she been forced to choose between Sam and Sid, she wouldn't have chosen her mother. Now, she was grateful to have her around.

She was also grateful that all this mess was at least happening now that they were established as a business. If a hiccup like this had happened with regular inventory before they opened, instead of with special inventory, they might not be here today, running her dream store.

So there were the positives.

But the negatives loomed large.

People were going to be here on a certain date to see this inventory whether she had it or not. If she didn't have it, word of mouth would not be too friendly toward the shop. People flying from all over, plane tickets purchased that couldn't be cancelled, hotel reservations made. That kind of negative publicity could shut them down.

Her neck started to itch. Hives. Stress hives. That hadn't happened to her since before Kevin's death. Kevin's ups and downs and the highs and lows of his depression used to trigger them. She tried not to scratch at her neck. She willed herself not to scratch at her neck. It had all been too easy, too perfect, and now came the reality check.

"Another letter," Matthew said and handed over the certified mail.

"Thanks." She took it and rubbed her eyes, then her temples.

He started to speak, but before he got a word out of his mouth, she said, "No, I'll take care of it."

He turned to leave, and she stopped him. "Oh, has anyone checked on Abby today?"

Sam

Lots of people live with their parents as adults, Sam thought to himself. *When you get down to it, it's not so much that I'm living with her as she's living with me.* How else do families take care of aging parents without shipping them off to a home? Sam was running through the go-to list of rationalizations he kept filed in the back of his mind for those occasions when he or someone else called his relationship with his mother into question. Right now was undoubtedly one of those occasions.

In truth, Sam knew that he'd never really gained the degree of independence that most men his age had, but he was a grown man and a damn good one at that. He may not have escaped his childhood home, but he had managed to start his own successful business in this town, and that was more than most people could say.

That's not what this is about, though, he admitted silently. *It's about character.*

Character meant a lot to Sam. Being someone of good character was more important than almost everything else. The problem with being of good character is that everyone expects you to please them after a while. Being a good person gets misconstrued with doing whatever it takes to make others happy. And it wasn't the same thing at all. Being a good person actually led to pissing people off a lot.

For starters, with Sidney. No, he wasn't going to abandon his mother and run for the hills just because she was needy and childish. She wouldn't understand the gesture. What would it solve?

And no, he wasn't going to ditch his girlfriend just because she didn't sit well with his mother. It wasn't about having his cake and eating it, too, either. It was about honoring his mother and trying to help her understand his needs and wants and about making an honest woman out of Sidney and protecting and cherishing her and their love despite both their mistakes. It was about being someone his nieces and nephews could look up to, since it was unlikely he'd ever have children of his own.

That was part of Sidney's appeal, to be honest. He loved kids, but he had never felt the calling or urge to be a father. He was a good caretaker, but he liked having his peace and quiet. Besides, he had sincere doubts he would even know how to begin. His own father hadn't made a very good show of it.

He'd told his mother this, and she'd been angry. She wanted proper grandchildren. She wanted Sam to find some young twenty-something and start popping them out. Sam had kicked himself for rolling his eyes at her, and not just because he got caught. He hated being someone who might roll his eyes at his mother. He should be better than that.

In any case, Sidney had a singular talent for making him furious. She knew exactly where the chinks in his armor were and precisely how to exploit them for maximum damage. But as angry as Sam was, he knew that for once in her life, Sidney wasn't coming from a wholly selfish and spiteful place. What she had said to him contained more than a grain of truth, and it was working on him like a pebble in his shoe.

"When were you thinking about cutting the cord, Sam? I would ask if you were planning on bringing her on the honeymoon, but it seems pointless, considering you've all but let her stop the wedding." Sidney glared at him and lit another cigarette. She closed her eyes in exasperation and tensely rubbed her left temple with her free hand.

When she opened her eyes and looked back into Sam's face, he could see the tears beginning to well and felt a painful squeeze in his chest.

"Do you love me, Sam?" she croaked.

"You know I do, Sid," he said, taking her hand from her face. "I've loved you since I was twelve years old."

"Do you want to be with me—marry me?"

"Of course I do. You know that."

"Then why can't you just do it?"

"Sid, it's not that simple." He knew it was a mistake the moment he said it. She yanked her hand from his as if she'd been burned, and her face twisted with rage. "What? How? How, Sam? How is this not ridiculously simple?" She turned from him, threw her cigarette in the sink, and walked out of the kitchen.

Sam followed her. He refused to let her walk out on the conversation, knowing that she was only a few steps behind walking out on him and everyone else. Sidney had always been a flight risk, and it hurt him deeply to know that after everything they'd been through since she'd returned to Lily Hollow, she would actually run again. There was no doubt in his mind that she had it in her, and it was at that moment that his own anger boiled over. "SIDNEY, YOU GET YOUR ASS BACK IN HERE!" He was shocked by the volume of his own voice, and by the way she jumped, he could tell that Sidney was, too, but only momentarily.

Matthew

Matthew's feet hit the floor, and immediately, he knew something was off. For starters, he had woken a full ten minutes before his alarm clock was due to go off. He had always been a sound—and sometimes late—sleeper, and as a result, he was forced to come to terms with the fact that he would never be one of those fortunate people who could rise early on their own. No, something had woken him.

Rain beat against his window at a sideways slant. The solid downpour of late had him bracing for a flash flood. Was it the storm? He waited a moment longer but didn't hear any thunder. He started to get out of bed and saw a pair of his boxers and one of his old T-shirts on the floor. He suddenly remembered that AJ had fallen asleep in his suite the night before, and it appeared that she'd left while he was still sleeping this morning. He got dressed quickly, combed his hair back haphazardly with water, and stepped out into the hall just in time to hear the first dish explode against the wall downstairs.

AJ came in the side entrance by the service elevator with her arm linked to Abigail Lacey's when something crashed in the café, causing her to jump. Broken plates?

Matthew was frozen in the stairwell between the second floor and the servant's entrance in the kitchen. He'd edged his way as close as he could before giving up in indecision. What should he do? Intervene? Let them fight it out? If they kept this up, he wouldn't have a café to open. Another dish clattered to the tile floor. Sam and Sidney were in the full throes of what sounded like a deal-breaking argument.

Sidney shouted, "You agreed with her! She said you would never actually marry me because you knew I was 'flighty.' Flighty! She said flighty! I am not flighty!"

Sidney was wildly strong willed, and she yelled when most people would probably cry. But living in such close quarters with his girlfriend's mother, he had learned her well and knew she was very, very hurt. "Flighty!" Sidney yelled again after a few seconds of silence.

Matthew raised his eyebrows. She was kidding herself if she actually believed that one. The woman was the very definition of flighty, but say that to her and you might lose an arm.

And Sam was indeed saying just that when AJ's voice piped in. "You two need to stop. Now. This is absurd."

Matthew eased himself into the room and stationed himself near Sam. He lightly touched his elbow and said, "Yeah, why don't we take a break, Sam?"

"Sidney, sit down," AJ told her mother. Sidney plopped herself on the kitchen stool for a half second, but when it looked as though Sam might move to step out back, she jumped up again.

"He does *not* get to leave this conversation! He is *not* walking out that door!"

Sam and Matthew froze, and seeing that they had listened and stayed, Sidney bolted from the kitchen.

"Oh noooo you don't!" Sam went after her, realizing her sole purpose of insisting he stay for the conversation was so that she could be the one to leave it.

He followed her through the café and into the bookstore area and reached for her arm.

"Yes, you are flighty. You get scared and you run. Maybe that's not how you see it from your perspective, being that Granddaddy Jack sent you packing the first time around, but it was an easy habit for you to get into. You run, and I still love you. But I won't sit around and wait for you to run out on me. I'm not the kid you babysit until you find you've got something better to do, and I'm not a doormat."

"That's fine. Fine! But I refuse to sit around waiting for a nearly forty-year-old man to make a decision without consulting his mother!" After that last burst, something in her face changed.

"I can't do this, Sam." All the fight had suddenly run out of her. Her posture deflated, and she turned her tired face to the floor.

No one said a word. There was a general sense of shock, not so much from what she had said, but the way she'd said it. Sidney was every inch a wildcat, and her sudden change had the entire room off balance.

And that was all she needed. "I'm so sorry, Sam—everyone. I'm so sorry." She was out the door and in the car before any of them could stop her.

Abigail

Fights had always been upsetting to Abigail, not just now that she was older. Not just now that she was rattled and easily confused.

She'd seen too many, said too little, and tried to be a peacemaker too often. This business with Sidney and Sam sent her reeling. If she knew where the girl had run off to, she'd stalk her down and tell her a thing or two. Life is too short to be so damn stubborn. She'd seen too many people be too stubborn. After all, wasn't it her own sister, Evie, who had written the book on it?

Part Two

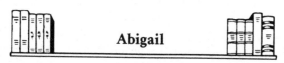

Abigail

"Jack Walters, if you enlist, I will never speak to you again," Evelyn said calmly. Her hand shook, holding her cigarette.

There was a patch of woods behind the hotel near the cemetery, and this is where they met to neck and spend time alone while Jack took breaks between the hotel guests' meal times. At the Lily Hollow Hotel, the bellhop was also the dining wait staff as well as the occasional laundry man. Evelyn would make the trip to the hotel in her best dress and carry the sheets and towels all the way back to the Lacey's house, where Olivia Lacey would wash and press everything. Often, Abigail had to help tote it all and spent many afternoons wandering the cemetery, waiting for Jack and Evie to finish with their stolen moments.

It was one of those afternoons. Abigail had come back to Jack and Evie's spot too soon and caught pieces of their conversation.

"I have to enlist. It would be un-American if I didn't. I want to go help. I can't sit at home and darn socks with you and Abby."

"Why can't you just call her Abigail? That's her name."

"And yours is Evelyn, and we all call you Evie."

"Abigail goes by Abigail, though. Stay home, Jack." For just an instant, her voice had taken on a whiny quality that was utterly unlike her. Abigail knew this would be the end of it. Part of her became jittery with excitement.

One thing about Evie was that if she said she'd never speak to someone again, she meant it. And Jack had to go to war. There was no question about it. So, if they never spoke, they couldn't get married. If they couldn't get married . . .

"I swear it, Jack Walters, if you go to war, we're done."

Jack didn't know Evelyn as well as he thought he did. From her hiding place, Abigail could see a hint of a smile creep up on his lips. The twinkle in his eye started to shine. He was flattered. This, he thought, was Evelyn's sign of love. She didn't want him to die in war. This, he believed, was her telling him she couldn't live without him.

He put his hands around her, and she awkwardly held on to the still-burning cigarette. "I mean it, Jack," she said.

"Evie," he whispered. Abigail couldn't hear him for sure, but she could suppose he was using that breathy voice he had when he was being tender and reassuring, saying something simple like, "I have to."

Evelyn jerked away from him and threw her cigarette at him. The rolled tobacco hit his shirt, and an ember burned a hole.

"Evie! You ruined my shirt!"

Normally, Evelyn might have shouted "Good!" over her shoulder, but she had vowed not to speak, so she didn't.

There were so many things about the last century that needed to stay in the last century, Abigail thought. Such a long life she had lived. And in that life, Jack had been a great many things. No one is any one particular thing or person. Everyone has shades and shadows and versions of themselves that different people bring out. Different relationships have different dynamics and cause you to react in ways you'd never believe.

She'd seen Jack do it. He hadn't always been the man AJ and Sidney knew. He hadn't even always been the man that Maude knew. Abigail wanted to protect Jack's secrets, like she always had. But she was following family tradition, she was losing her good sense, she was growing old, and she needed help.

What Maude knew or didn't know was beyond Abigail, but there were two things Abigail didn't want: to leave her beloved home or to accidentally share any information that would cause Maude to doubt her deceased father. So Abigail was determined to stay in her own house until she was found dead. No one needed to hear the babbling she knew was yet to come. No one needed to help her to the bathroom. She'd rather suffer in her own filth. She didn't want any of Jack's children to experience the horror of finding her with her pants sullied like she had found Uncle Ollie years ago.

Logically, though, she knew they would never let her stay alone. And she knew what to expect. She could give them lists. Taking her to the bathroom every thirty minutes like a toddler would be it.

How had this happened?

She'd been a caretaker her whole life, and now she felt helpless. And time just stretched on. *Can I go now, please?* she asked God. *Please?* For the first time in her life, she questioned why her sister had done it—jumped off that bridge. She'd always thought she'd known. But now, she wondered if Evie had just understood her own mind better than anyone could have imagined.

After all, why pair yourself up with another suicidal? Why deny yourself the peace and love of a good man like Jack? Why jump off a bridge at twenty-two? Why leave your lover alone in the world to sit and brood in his misery? Back then, Abigail had felt relief over Evie's death, but now she wondered if she, Abigail, had been the selfish one all along.

After all, there were long periods of time in Abigail's life that she only recalled in slow motion, and they were mostly the days after Evie's death. Why? Because it was when she felt as though Jack was slipping away from her.

Imagine that.

Losing a sister and being more concerned about the attention of a man than grieving her absence. Ironically, those were the days Jack had relied on her most, and it was long after knowing he was never in her grasp.

She had come to the house every day promptly at eight, picked up Maude, and left Jack to his own devices. Maude sat at the Laceys' bakery, before Abigail had put her own first name on the sign, and ate quiche and tarts for breakfast each morning. Maude seemed to understand the gravity of the situation, because she remained a solemn and easy-to-manage child. Abigail tucked her into a corner table, and the little girl drew pictures.

She wasn't very imaginative, but her attention to detail was startling for a person so young. At five, Maude could recreate the bakeshop in shocking detail. With her pencils, she scrawled people walking by, and though they were nowhere near perfect portraits, Abigail could always tell which town member had taken a stroll down Main Street that day.

After she was done at the bakery for the day, she would lock up and take Maude for a picnic. Sometimes, as she bolted the door, she would catch a glimpse of Jack coming in or out of the hotel, but most days, he stayed at home and let the place run itself. Regardless, Abigail and Maude would march through the grass in the empty lot nearest the hotel, Maude stepping carefully so as to not get into any ant piles or catch nettles on her skirts. So different from what Abigail remembered of her own childhood spent chasing butterflies and swimming in mud holes.

When Abigail had been really young, the whole Lacey family had had ritual picnics every week. The few memories she had of her father and oldest brother were a hodgepodge of family gatherings in fields of wildflowers down the road from their house. Mama would lay out a patchwork quilt and pass around little sandwiches with lemonade in the picnic china. Evie always sat off on her own, despondent, barely nibbling her food, but drinking all the lemonade as though she were the queen of England. Their brother John Jr. and Jack Walters were the only people who could tear Evie away from herself, and even then, she only half ran when games began.

Jack always chased and flirted when he joined them. Abigail remembered taking turns being lifted high on his and her father's shoulders. *Why couldn't he behave so wonderfully with his own child?* Abigail had wondered while watching Maude pace slowly up and down a path, inspecting the ants hard at work, or when she was older, fussing with the picnic items in silence. So very different from the laughter and play of the Laceys.

It was on those days, watching Maude, that Abigail tried hard to summon Emma to mind, the wisp of a girl who'd had the honor and curse of being Jack Walters's wife, if only for a while. She'd been a quiet thing, but not a haughty quiet like Evie. She'd just smiled and enjoyed the world. Every now and then, the little waif would cough a few times and vanish to another room or behind a tree if they were outside.

In the summers, Emma wore large, wide-brimmed hats and hid in the shade. She was pale and burned easily in the sun. Evie seemed to oppose her at every chance and would lay herself out on rocks, soaking in the rays with a deathlike stare at Jack.

"She'll really never speak to me, will she?" Jack had asked Abigail at a church potluck on the lawn one day.

Abigail had squinted over the grass and the children fighting over cotton candy. Emma had been tucked in the cool shade of an oak tree, nursing Maude. Abigail had shifted her gaze a bit and saw Evie perched on a picket fence, her skirt billowing in the breeze, sharing a cigarette with her husband as he talked to her. She didn't even seem aware of him. Instead, her eyes burned a hole into Jack Walters, so much that he broke into a sweat and peeled his suit jacket off his shoulders.

"She said she wouldn't, so she won't," Abigail said to him. "What's it matter? You have Emma and Maude now."

"It matters." Jack tossed the coat over his shoulder, and without taking his eyes off Evie, he stalked over to the tree, sat down, and kissed Emma's cheek. Emma just smiled at her husband, and they played with the baby together a moment.

Evie had responded by tapping her cigarette, taking another drag, and flicking it away. She had hopped off the fence and immediately left the church.

Who were these people Abigail loved so much? What game did they think they were playing?

Maude

Maude had been so young when Emma died, no one could imagine she remembered her mother at all, yet there were times when Maude, while out in town, would come across some frail older woman and felt a strong sense of familiarity as if she should be able to place the stranger somehow. Surely that was a memory.

Although Maude had known Abigail Lacey her entire life and Abigail had always been a complete saint to their family, there were moments when Maude caught a glimpse of her from the corner of her eye and physically shuddered. She didn't understand this feeling until she was in her teens. She was alone at the house snooping through Jack's writing room when she was in high school and found pictures tucked away that she had never seen before and would never see again.

She spotted her mother and Abigail smiling brightly, and she saw her baby self perched on Jack's hip, all quite as expected. The part that startled her was her father's faraway look as he gazed over the head of his wife, past Abigail, to a woman who looked shockingly like Miss Abby. She was a little taller, a little older, and a little sharper in every way. She wasn't as soft as Abigail, she was a bit bony, and her expression was not kind. She seemed painfully aware of Jack's gaze and looked as though she had begun to move outside of the shot of the camera when it went off.

That was when Maude's father walked in. Maude sensed him stiffen in the doorframe. She, too, was often painfully aware of his presence and his distance.

"Who is that, Daddy?"

"Evelyn Rhys. Her husband was taking the picture." He didn't even have to cross the room and look to know what she was talking about.

"Who was she?"

"Abby's older sister." Until then, Maude wasn't consciously aware that Abigail Lacey had ever had an older sister. Maude knew about an older brother and a few family ties to the Rhys', as Abigail always claimed Karl and his wife as her nephew and niece—Karl the son of a third cousin or some sort of small town familial nonsense—but she didn't know about this sister. Later, she would remember the knowledge, but it would take Evie a long time to be reborn in Maude's mind.

"Why does no one talk about her?"

"She killed herself."

"And Mr. Rhys?"

"He died shortly before she did."

Maude looked back at the woman, dressed out of her time, wearing long beads around her neck and her hair fashioned to the jazz age. "She looks strange."

"She was something else. Put those away. I don't want them out."

Jack didn't speak to her again for days. He poured himself into a novel—one of his better selling ones—and Maude spent the week in solitude, a common practice in their house.

Out of curiosity, she took a few hours to walk the Lily Hollow cemetery and stumbled across Evelyn Rhys. She wasn't buried in the Rhys family plot next to her husband, but instead was next to an Esme Olivia Lacey, born the same day. The stones were joined by two iron cherubs on a cast iron trellis. Jasmine grew up the metal grate.

The cherubs were unusually gothic and almost had a fairy or pixie quality to them. Their faces weren't round and fat like the other cherubs in the cemetery. Instead, they were pointed and looked a little sinister.

"I never see you out here," Abigail said, interrupting Maude's thoughts.

"There's not much use visiting the dead," Maude said. "They aren't here." Even as a teenager, she had little sentiment toward those who weren't around.

"It makes me feel better to give a good talking to my sisters. My brother, too." She pointed to a grave on the other side of Esme—John Lacey, Jr. Behind them, inside the little fence line, were much smaller stones for a John and Olivia Lacey. Not too far off was an Oliver Blythe.

"What was Evelyn like?"

"Harsh. Excitable."

"And Daddy, back then?"

"He smiled more. Became smitten easily. He was calm and steady, the most loving soul of anyone in Lily Hollow."

That wasn't how Maude felt about him. He was quiet and distant, but she supposed he was easier than most fathers.

"So, who are you going to the dance with?" Abigail changed the subject and began to lead Maude away from the dead and gone. "That Montgomery boy ask you yet?"

"No. Is he planning on it?"

"So says his mother. He's quite taken with you."

Maude couldn't imagine why. Henry Montgomery was full and muscular, with a fine jaw. He kept his slightly auburn hair slicked back to show light freckles along his forehead. She knew his face well. She'd drawn it so many times. Why would a boy like that think twice about a girl like her? She was tall for a girl, and bony. She imagined she looked exactly like her father had at fifteen, but finding pictures of him from then was nearly impossible.

"You do look like Jack," Abigail said, reading her mind. "That's a good thing. He always was a handsome boy."

But I'm not a boy, Maude thought. She forced a smile in appreciation of the compliment anyway.

Even the idea of Henry Montgomery asking her to a dance couldn't distract Maude from the idea of Evelyn Rhys. The knowledge of the woman itched at her. Usually a very focused student, Maude couldn't think in school, and one day she decided she'd just have another look.

Maude sneaked back into her father's study and looked for more pictures, but it seemed Jack had hidden everything she had seen just a few days before. At least she thought so, until she found an old shoe-box tucked under a floorboard.

The loose board was under Jack's desk. She heard the rattle under her foot when she sat down in his chair in frustration, ready to give up. She gave it an extra tap with her toe as she bent down to listen. The board popped up, revealing a hidey-hole and the box. It was covered in brown shipping paper and had an address torn away from the top. It had come to her father by mail, it seemed.

She opened the top and was surprised to find it filled to the brim with letters—old, yellowed things that had been read and re-read. The handwriting was old and elegant, done with a fine fountain pen, it looked like. The folds and creases in some of them were beginning to tear from age and handling.

Maude checked the clock. He wouldn't be home for hours. It was his late day at the hotel. She fingered the items of the box gingerly before diving in and flipping through them. Some were dated, and some were not.

Jack,

I saw you today buying groceries at the market. I know you saw me too because you flipped that red apple in your pocket just to tease me. As if thievery would compel me to speak to you. What a laugh!

Do you remember the first time old man MacGregor caught us? Of course you do. You'll never kiss me like that again, Jack Walters, not out in public in the world. You should have listened when I told you not to leave me.

Ronald bought me new pens for our anniversary. Jealous? Of course you are.

No longer yours,

Evie

Evie. Abgail's sister. The woman in the photo looking at her father who was married with a baby on his hip. What a horrid woman! Maude looked at the date. Her mother was still alive when this was written! Though it was probably before that picture was taken. But it was only a scrap of paper, not full stationery.

It seemed, as Maude took a closer inspection of the contents of the box, that nothing was in a proper envelope. She found notes scrawled on book pages ripped from their binding, on torn grocery bag paper, and even scrawled on a receipt.

The receipt itself was faded. Maude could barely make out the letter "S" in a curlycue font, and the rest was gone with age. On the back, Evie had written,

It's not the same without you. – E

Finally, she found the thickest of the bunch. It was on a sheet of very expensive paper, like the kind at Gloria's Stationery Store in Briar. Soft and fine like cotton, with tiny gold peacock feathers embossed on the edges.

My Dearest Jack,

I told you I would never speak to you again, and so I haven't. Are you proud of me for keeping a promise? You know your Evie—if nothing at all, I am at least a woman of my word when I want to be . . .

Oh my words . . .

All of them withheld these years. I penned and kept them here for you. They needed an outlet, you see. They needed to leave my mind so that I could at least pretend they would reach you somehow. Divine intervention, if you believe in that sort of thing. Maybe by witchcraft and sorcery. The townies would love that, if I turned out to be a witch. Would you defend me? Confess that you know firsthand there are no marks of the devil on this flesh?

Ronald has shot himself. Although we both know I led him to do it. I didn't love him and he always knew and now he's not even cold in the next room and I'm writing a letter to my lover. Don't worry, my love, I'll hide it before the authorities get here. I have nothing to fear; I did not pull the trigger. Though I might have if he had continued on the way he has been. He always cries, you know. I cannot stand a man who cries. Though, I'll forgive you if you cry for me. I might even enjoy it a bit.

I've missed you, darling, don't forget that. I have. I've miss-ed you every day. And I'm sure now that Emma is gone, you'll be expecting me to run to your arms when you find out Ronald is stone dead. I won't be doing that.

You have that child. As Abigail can attest, I am no good with children. You love it and would expect me to love it as well. I just wouldn't, you know.

So when you get this, I'll be gone. You know why, my love. I hear Esme calling me every day now. We are soul mates, you see, Esme and I, separated by the ether. I see her clearest in the water, and she finds me in the ripples.

I suppose next you see me, you'll be staring down from the bridge. I imagine myself a bit like Ophelia. Though I must confess, I never read that one, either. You talked about it often enough, and I am certain Abigail read it for you. Always your little follower.

I will never follow you, Jack Walters. I am not weak like Abigail. She may tread on your shadow forever, but it will be as you chase me. The thought of it should not make me laugh, but it does.

I should want Abigail to be happy. I should want you to be happy. But I don't, my darling, I want you to both live a marvelously miserable life together. You long for me, and she'll long for you . . .

It's all her fault, after all. We would be together if she hadn't been in the woods that day, always watching. If she hadn't been there, I wouldn't have threatened you so harshly. But little Abigail couldn't witness me beg. Never. So I said I'd never speak to you again, and I didn't. When you are old and gray and bitter about it all, remember how young and beautiful I will always be and that everything bad in your life was all because little Abigail Lacey followed us into the woods.

I suppose Ronald is cold enough now that there is no chance of anyone saving him. I should muster up a bit of hysteria so I can call the police. Or should I just call the funeral home? What would a truly hysterical and loving wife do? I should wait to make my decisions until I've become altogether hysterical. I'll know instinctively how to be irrational then.

I love you, darling,

Always with every fiber of my being,

Forever yours, Evie

Folded over herself, in that way tall girls often do when they are young and insecure, Maude hid in her room at the front of the house. She shouldn't have read those letters. After the last one, she'd stuffed them all back in the box in tears and slid the floorboard back into place. She hid in her room, waiting for her father to arrive. She had double-checked everything to be sure it was as she had found it, but she was still certain he would somehow notice something out of place.

She had a sharp eye for those details. She could tell, for instance, when Abigail visited the house in their absence, even before the faint-est smell of baked cookies reached her nose from the kitchen. Abigail had a key, and when she came to the house, there was just something in the air to say someone had been there. It wasn't as stale; the house didn't seem lonely.

On top of that, there was the garden feud to note evidence of. Jack Walters liked plants to work for their water. He said if you gave it to them moderately, it forced their roots to dig deeper for the moist soil far under the earth. Abigail, on the other hand, couldn't stand the sight of a near-thirsty plant and carefully drizzled water over the gardens when she came by after closing the bakery for the day.

When Maude came home from school, she always checked the plants. If they looked limp from a hard day in the sun, she knew there'd be no after-school snack, but if they looked perky—a little less thirsty—then she knew there would be cookies, or tarts, or a pie. Jack never noticed the difference, but Maude sure did.

Maude could also tell from the second she hit the gate whether the postman had come that day. The mailbox hung off the front porch. It wasn't at the end of the drive like at the newer houses in Lily Hollow. When the postman came, he opened the front gate, sauntered up the drive, and headed back out. He always left the gate only half latched, though. In his hurry to move to the next house, he didn't pull the gate behind him with enough force. Abigail told her once that she should be a police detective. Maude had only smiled a little.

The truth was, Maude wasn't sure what she wanted out of life. She had no desire to be a writer like her father, although she'd met his publisher a few times and he'd asked her if she had any material. Her father said the hotel was hers one day if she wanted it, but all she could ask was, "What would I do with it?"

"Anything you want, Maude. It's a beautiful building with a lot of history. It doesn't have to stay a hotel. You could make it an art museum!" He nodded toward her sketchbook.

She unconsciously cradled the book as if it were a child in danger of being snatched. She didn't want anyone to see her drawings, ever. She wasn't fearful of peoples' responses. They were good—she knew that. They were just hers. Handing over her drawings to the public eye would be like handing over a diary. Besides, what would Lily Hollow do with an art gallery anyway?

She heard the gate click, and she threw herself onto her bed and lifted her head above the headboard just high enough to peer out the window behind it. It faced the front yard, and she saw her father in the slacks and shirt he wore most often heading up the sidewalk.

He looked absent minded as usual, so much so that when he entered the front door, he forgot to even announce his arrival. Maude emerged from her room just as he was about to enter his office.

"Hungry?" she asked.

"Oh, hi, Maude. Yes, dinner would be nice."

She went to the kitchen and busied herself with chicken breast and green beans, straining to hear if he found anything amiss in his office. If he did, he didn't let on.

While the chicken was in the oven and the green beans soaked up bacon on the stove, she set the timer and tiptoed back to her room. She suddenly had an image to get out of her head, and she wasn't going to safely get it out in the kitchen.

As she started to sketch, she realized it was a memory from her childhood, a very early one. The image had come to mind before as possibly her earliest memory. She'd always thought it was Abigail, but as her pencil caressed the paper in long, quick strokes, she realized

what she should have known all along. This wasn't Abigail. This was
a woman who looked a lot like Abigail but detested Maude's very existence.

The woman was crouched before her, peering into her eyes. A
peacock feather lay in her hair as though it had just fallen from the
sky and nestled there, finally at home. As her face emerged from the
hairline, Maude realized she was much prettier than Abigail. And
younger—at least younger than Abigail was now. The pencil lingered around the mouth, and Maude could hear the woman saying,
"Give this to your mommy."

But she couldn't remember what she handed her. It had to be something small, something fit for the tiny hands of a child. But what?

When Henry Montgomery asked Maude to the prom, she had the
end of a pencil in her mouth and was lost in a math problem. Lost
because Evie's face was haunting her and she desperately wanted to
pull out her sketchbook, but it was safely tucked away.

"Maude," he said. "Maude."

She looked up at him as he leaned over her table in the cafete-
ria. She pulled the pencil from her lip, startled. Her back straightened as she slipped the pencil behind her ear and turned to give him
her full attention, but as he leaned closer, she slouched into herself
and tucked her forearms into her long legs.

"Yes?" she asked when he didn't continue.

"I'd like to take you to the dance."

"Yes?"

"So is that a yes?"

"Oh, yes."

"Great."

It took a minute, but she finally remembered to smile. Abigail
had been right. He did like her, but she couldn't imagine why. They
couldn't be more different. He was a stocky wrestling captain, and
she was a tall mathlete who spent more time sketching portraits of
her teachers in the margins of her notes. She would feel the same

way when he asked her to marry him. Come to think of it, it went about the same as his prom proposal.

"Maude? I'd like to marry you."

"Yes?"

"Is that a yes?"

"Oh, yes."

And then he kissed her.

It was Abigail who took Maude to Briar to look for a dress, of course. They walked quietly through various shops. Abigail's only advice was that Maude would look nice in blue. Maude ran her hands across the racks—silks, cottons, lace, which one should she choose?

She settled on one that was a bit of all three. A cotton A-line with a second layer of lace and a satin sash for the waist. The cotton and satin were a light blue, and the white lace draped like an apron along the skirt.

"This one."

"It's truly lovely, Maude. Go try it on."

Sidney

Sidney didn't make it far when she left after her last fight with Sam. She hadn't really intended to. She just wanted to take a walk. The walk turned into a drive, the suitcase—her ever-present "go-bag"—in her trunk reminding her how easy it was to leave. The car took her to Briar. Within an hour, after circling the square about a thousand times, she found herself parked in front of a cute little row of townhomes that had evolved into businesses over the years. One was a bed and breakfast, and she went inside and asked for a key.

The lady at the counter swiped her credit card, handed her some papers to sign, and gestured to the living area. "Help yourself to any of the many books in our library."

Sidney turned her head and glanced at the two small bookshelves in the living room. A tabby cat rolled over on the floor, stretched his legs and claws, and meowed. Sidney rolled her eyes. This lady had no idea what "many books" meant. Sidney hadn't, either, before the Bookshop Hotel, not really. Even Granddaddy Jack, the avid reader, had only kept one bookshelf in the house. He'd mostly utilized Lily Hollow's very small library. When he had bought books, he'd had a tendency to donate them to the library when he was done with them, because Lily Hollow didn't have much in the way of a library budget.

Ugh. She didn't want to think about books or Lily Hollow or anything.

"No, thanks," she said. The politeness in her own voice surprised her. She'd grown accustomed to saying thank you and no thank you and being mannerly and polite around Matthew, AJ, and Sam, because they were polite with each other—because they expected it from others. Years of traveling the world prior, she hadn't really been that polite of a person. She'd been polite when she wanted something from someone, not just for the sake of being polite. She smiled at the girl to cover her train of thought.

"Will you be in Briar long?" the clerk asked.

"No, just doing some weekend shopping, I think."

"Candice's is nice. It's my favorite."

"Thank you. I'll try to go check it out." Sidney's bag was still in the car. She didn't bother taking it up to her room yet. She pocketed the key away in her purse and headed out on foot. She knew Briar well enough and had been to Candice's many times. A new dress might be just what she needed, and Candice's always had a fun assortment of second-hand designer dresses.

When Sidney thought back to all her shopping excursions, one in particular came to mind. She was ten years old and had just gotten her ears pierced. Maude had pierced them for her in the kitchen with a giant needle, a bar of soap, and nothing to numb the pain. Her mother had told her if she wanted to be beautiful and extravagant so badly, she'd need to pay the price for that beauty and extravagance and that oftentimes, that meant it would hurt a little. Sidney had been so excited to finally have pierced ears, she hadn't even felt it. Maude had put in studs to keep the holes fresh, and then, six weeks later, Abigail had taken her shopping for a pair of dangly earrings.

"This is where you'll find the best earrings," Abigail had told her as she marched her into a little boutique in a garage apartment of a woman's house on Rose of Sharon Boulevard. "Charisse makes all the jewelry herself."

Oh, Abigail. Was anyone checking on her right now? Did she need someone to prattle to? Sidney hadn't had a second thought other than getting out of town for a few days, but now she wondered what those few days could mean to others. It had become Sidney's job to fetch her from her home every morning and get her to the bakery if she was lucid or to the bookshop if she wasn't. Everyone had a job to do right now. Everyone was a cog in a machine that was the daily routine of Abigail's life right now. Who was going to pick up the slack Sidney had left?

Maude

Maude was picking up Sidney's slack. She was her mother, after all. It was her job, her duty. She'd always picked up after Sidney, cleaned up the messes she'd left behind. Why would now be any different? She'd raised AJ when Sidney had flitted off to see the world, so of course Maude would now be looking after Abigail in the mornings.

Truth be told, though, she was glad to do it. She'd been feeling a little left out with nothing to do since Daddy had died and that old building had started taking up everyone's time. She had expressed being happy to finally have the house to herself, to finally have her own life to herself. At first, she was. She was stubborn and wanted to stick to that sentiment, but really, it was lonely being her own person after a life of being everyone else's helper.

She'd been Daddy's helper her whole life. The town loved him, but they didn't realize how useless he could be, getting wrapped up in his head and his work. She'd been a mother to her daughter and then again to her granddaughter. Now she was mothering Abigail some days. The logical step would be to do what AJ kept hinting at, take Abigail in and let someone buy Abby's old house.

Maude loved Abigail. It would be a privilege to have her in her home. It would also be admitting defeat. She couldn't live not taking care of someone, not literally cleaning up someone's messes. She didn't know what to do with herself. She had no hobbies of her own except her artwork that no one ever saw. She had been looking forward to maybe setting up Daddy's old office as a drawing room. But she couldn't do that with Abigail lurking about. Could she? Maude hated people looking at her art.

She should put her foot down, assert boundaries. She had her own life. She was an old woman! She deserved her own life! Even as she thought it, she knew it wasn't entirely true. Even as she thought it, she knew Abigail would be moving into the Walter-Montgomery home sooner or later.

Montgomery. She'd carried the name for so many years, it hardly meant anything anymore. Once, it had meant so much. She thought of her Henry and how quickly he had been taken from her.

Maude walked into her room, the room she'd had at that house her whole life, aside from the few brief years she'd lived with Henry on the military base. She reached under the bed and touched one of the many boxes with her fingertips, pulling the one within reach out and onto the bedspread. Tucked inside were a sketchpad and assorted pencils and erasers.

Her bones hurt too much to spread out on the bed like she had as a girl. Instead, she propped the pad up in the windowsill at the head of the bed and drew while sitting upright. She'd sketched this front lawn more times than she could count. Her sketchpads had seen every season, every variation of flowers in the gardens. The mailbox in sunshine and in snow, the sidewalk with dancing squirrels and feisty cardinals. Pictures of Henry, Granddaddy Jack, AJ, Sidney—all of their faces were captured in time under that bed in boxes.

From memory, Maude sketched a younger Abigail walking up the sidewalk to the front door.

Abigail

Little Maude came to Abigail and sat down in her lap. Abigail wrapped her arms around the girl, and they enjoyed looking out into the garden. Emma was inside the house, locked up like a mummy in a tomb, wasting away while Jack stood guard. A tiny hand met Abigail's, and a dusty but smooth oblong object was tucked shyly into her palm. Abigail absently looked down to see what treasure the toddler had found and was gifting, undoubtedly only to take it back again in a moment.

It was a peanut.

Emma Walters was highly allergic to peanuts, an ailment that made it very difficult to keep her healthy if you were to add it to all her other little weaknesses. Jack, an avid lover of peanut butter, had to rid the house of it. Abigail had to stop making any kind of treats for the bakery that included the ingredient.

The whole town was on constant alert to be sure that Emma Walters never encountered peanuts, peanut butter, peanut oil—any of it. Her peanut allergy was so severe, even the pastor's wife had to stop making peanut brittle for the church's Thanksgiving feast, as Emma couldn't be in the same building with it or shake hands with someone who had touched it.

"Maude, where did you get this?"

"The lady at the gate."

"What did the lady at the gate say?"

"For Mommy!" the girl said.

"No, Maude. You must never ever give something like this to your mommy." Abigail got up and threw the peanut far over the fence. She stripped the girl down to her panties and started hosing her down in the garden. Once she had sufficiently cleaned Maude, she scrubbed at her own hands under the water before going inside and dumping the confused child in a bath.

"What happened?" Jack asked, frantic to see Abigail so distraught. She was holding Maude, naked and wrapped in towels, close to her damp breast. Bits of wet hair pressed against her skin, stuck by the moisture.

"Nothing, Jack. Nothing. I've taken care of it." She was surprised he hadn't heard the baby scream when the cold water rushed out of the hose and smacked against her skin. Abigail had been so terrified, she'd just begun spraying water everywhere. It wasn't until her skirt became soaked from the backsplash that she had realized she needed to get the child into a warm bath.

Then there was that rainy day so long ago. Abigail's hair had started coming undone from the pins when Jack stepped out of the car. How many times would this man see her disheveled by water? she remembered thinking when the car screeched to a halt in front of her.

"Abby! What are you doing in the rain? In the middle of the road?"

"She's dead, Jack. Evie's dead." She knew this would break his heart. It was her sister, but she cried now because it was Jack who would feel hurt by this the most.

"What happened?"

"She jumped off McGregor Bridge."

Jack sucked in his breath. Rain dripping down his nose surged toward his lips with the inhale.

"Evie's dead?"

"Evie's dead."

It was too much too soon. Jack had just buried Emma, Evelyn had just survived her husband's suicide, and now here they all were again, except not.

Abigail stood on the road, soaked with rain and the realization that Jack had been headed out to Evelyn's.

"We were going to be together. Why would she do it? She was free of him."

"Did she actually say that, Jack?"

"No. She hadn't said a word."

Abigail had nothing to say to him. Maude was in the back seat screeching up a storm, and Abby went to the car and sat with the little girl.

"Daddy crying?"

"He's sad, Maude, that's all."

"Why?"

"My sister died."

"You sad?"

"I am."

Abigail pulled the door shut and held Maude's little hand while she watched Jack out the window. He had collapsed there in the gravel and mud as the rain washed over him. It was the only time in all her years that Abigail would make no effort to comfort him.

The child's hand seemed to grow in her own, and Abigail looked down at her fingers entwined with an adult's. It was Maude's grand-daughter, AJ, holding on to her, patting the top of her veined skin with her free hand. She had lost herself again.

"There are so many things I never told you, AJ. Never told anyone for that matter."

AJ turned to Abigail. "Oh?"

"Did you know I had a sister?"

"No, I didn't."

"Two, actually, but I never met one. Evelyn and Esme were twins. Twins ran in my Mama's family, you know. Every generation, it seemed, had a pair. Evie was the sister I grew up with. Your granddad Jack was so in love with her."

AJ's eyebrows arched. "You mean Emma? Grandma Emma?"

"No. I mean Evelyn, my sister. Emma was a frail and good-hearted woman Jack felt sorry for and brought home after the war. After she died, I think he fell in love with the idea of her, but Evie was his true love. She's a relative of your late husband. She was Mrs. Ronald Rhys."

"She married into Kevin's family?"

"Oh yes, but you know the Rhys' better than anyone. Ronald was a lot like your Kevin. He was nice and all most of the time, but he and Evie deserved each other."

Evelyn, of course, had had her wedding at the hotel. It was the thing to do back then. All of the highest society was having parties and weddings at the old hotel just like they had in the twenties, before the Depression and the war.

If Abigail were to marry, she wanted it proper, in the church, like Mama and Daddy had. But Evie had never cared for what was good and proper, only what seemed rich and exciting.

The Rhys family had even paid for Evie to have the most fashionable of dresses, doing everything to have a wedding they thought they'd never see.

Abigail stood in a pale yellow dress. Evie had wanted yellow, lots of yellow, so Abigail wore yellow. No one knew why. Yellow was not a color Evie had ever particularly favored, and she was not known to ever use it again in her décor or dress. But she insisted, and Abigail and her mother had slaved night and day over tiny little yellow cream puffs and a wedding cake draped with yellow roses and took extra care to find material for yellow dresses, which was just as well to Abigail. She knew it was a color Jack liked to see on ladies. He thought it made them look "like spring and summer all rolled into one," she recalled him saying once.

Jack stood across from her, popping a puff in his mouth. "These are delicious," he said, cream cheese icing spilling to the corners of his lips.

"Where's Emma?" Abigail looked around.

"Not feeling well. The baby is due any day, and she's been in bed all week. My mother is with her. She says hello and to save a dance for you."

Abigail clasped her hands together in angst. Emma was so kind and dear, which made it all the more difficult to hate her. Jack had found the sweetest wife anyone could find, and it took all Abigail had to not wish she was a terrible human so she could be hated. But when it came right to it, Abigail was happy that Jack was happy. That's why it pained her when Evie came out in her extravagant dress and was announced as Mr. and Mrs. with her new spouse but looked over her new husband's shoulder as he spun her on the dance floor and shot Jack a look that paled him.

It was then that Abigail fully realized Evie's desire for yellow in the wedding. The yellow roses and baby's breath draped throughout her hair made her look innocent and bridal. It made Jack's eyes light up as she spun in her dress on the dance floor while his wife was tucked away in bed with the windows drawn, hidden away from the light.

"So how about it, Abby?" He turned from Evie's taunting gaze and took Abigail's hand. "Care for a dance?"

How could she say no? She could feel the blush coming on and breathed deeply to make it subside. When Jack took her hand, his soft fingers felt strange against her leathered skin. Years of laundry and baking had made them rough and unladylike before she'd left her teens.

It should have been wonderful, a high. Instead, Abigail kept thinking of Emma at home ready to pop with their first child. Jack kept his eyes on the newlyweds and seemed out of sorts when Abigail tried to talk to him about the number of people in attendance and whether any of the other young people would be getting married soon.

Ronald Rhys whisked Evie away to New York for their honeymoon. They stayed in posh hotels, went to Broadway shows, and spent entire evenings out dancing. The Rhys family had some of the oldest money in Lily Hollow—aside from the Carsons—and Ronald received his trust fund upon his marriage. Gossips around town accused Evie of marrying him for his money, because everyone was certain she and Jack Walters were destined for the altar. But Abigail knew that Evie was in it for spite more than she could ever be for money.

When Ronald and Evie came home from their month away from Lily Hollow, Evie didn't see it fitting to live in town. Instead, she convinced Ronald to buy a chunk of the MacGregors' land across the Mac-Gregor bridge. An old farming family, they owned pretty much all the acreage between Lily Hollow and Briar, including a large portion of woods people referred to as the Blackbriar Forest.

The MacGregors had chronic money troubles, and every decade or so, a MacGregor would sell off another plot of the wooded portion to some family or another, mostly to the older families in the area who wanted to preserve the land and keep it out of the hands of developers.

Though they ran the market, the MacGregors kept to themselves more often than not. They were a steady and frugal family by necessity and, living in between city limits, didn't really belong to Lily Hollow but didn't really belong to Briar, either. They were nice people. Everyone generally liked them, but they were never really involved in much.

Living in no-man's-land appealed to Evie. She relished the feeling of otherworldliness, of not quite belonging anywhere.

The walk from the Lacey's little bungalow to Ronald and Evie's estate was at least an hour. By car, it wasn't far at all, but Abigail never went anywhere by car back then. Her mother had sent her to Evie's with a sack of extra potatoes from the garden, certain the newlyweds would starve without her care packages. After all, Evie wouldn't cook, she had a bad habit of killing anything she touched, and she couldn't stand being dirty.

The canvas sack was already beginning to dig into Abigail's shoulder by the time she hit Swan Lane, and just as she noticed it, a pebble found its way into her shoe from the dirt road. Why did Evie have to be so difficult? As soon as the estate was complete, she'd become bored with it and have Ronald drop a million on something else, no doubt. The potatoes lay in the canvas bag in the middle of the road—probably bruised—as Abigail fished the rock out from under her heel. Evie deserved bruised potatoes if she wasn't willing to plant them herself.

It shouldn't be Mother's job to feed them while they spent more money than God himself had on a ridiculous castle. That's what Evie was calling it when she came to have lunch with them one day, anyway. "Ronald's building me a castle," she kept saying.

Abigail shouldered the potatoes again and decided to leave the road. It would be another mile or so before the split came, but if she cut across the field into the woods now, she'd emerge directly at the ravine and the MacGregor Bridge. Abigail used to love coming out to the bridge as a child, mostly to play, but sometimes she'd take a pole and pull a few small river fish out and take them home to Mother to cook for dinner.

The tall grass tickled her knees as she cut herself a path. The sun bore down overhead and threatened to burn her nose. Tiny yellow butterflies flitted around the field, moving en masse from the south for the sole purpose of chasing dandelion puffs in Lily Hollow. Once disturbed, the puffs broke into a thousand pieces, got caught by the

wind, and danced their way into Abigail's hair. It was one of her favorite seasons. She sighed.

Truth be told, every season was one of her favorite seasons. She
always found desirable reasons to be out of doors. Usually, the only
thing that kept her in all day was her passion for baking. She began to
daydream a bakery with an outdoor kitchen. Wouldn't that be lovely?
To bake tarts in the crisp dewy morning of fall and winter, the heat
from the oven clashing with the cool of the air against your skin.

This thought came to her just as the cool of the wood met her
warm cheeks. The change from sun to the shade was welcome, and
she quickly found the existing deer path that she used to find her way
to the bridge. Out of the field, she plucked off her shoes and went barefoot. The patted-down earth was nearly cold against her toes, and she
smiled with delight.

Why was Evie the one who'd moved to the woods? Allowing herself to drift into whimsy in the calm of the forest, Abigail imagined
a small cottage on a plot of land just beyond that tree. She eyed an
especially tall oak. Or that tree. She noted an aspen sheltering a nest of
some kind. Her imaginary cottage was made of humble stone, perhaps
plucked from the ravine, though she didn't want to disturb nature too
much. It had wooden shutters and no windowpanes. There was a tiny
chimney blowing ginger-scented smoke out of the roof.

The inside held a large Dutch oven, a cozy bedroom with a heavy
quilt over the bed, and a little writing room off to the side. Buried
under a pile of books and a bright imagination was Jack. It was a quiet,
simple daydream, but it was pure perfection. She imagined bringing
him coffee and Danish rolls in the morning and milk and cookies in
the afternoon. She even gloried in the idea of getting him a little pudgy
from all the sugar she would feed him. It would do him good to gain
a few pounds.

At least it wasn't Jack whom Evie had dragged into the trees—Abigail's precious trees. She wouldn't have been able to bear it. She was at
peace with Jack's choice in Emma. She was quiet and kind. And Evie
could brood out here with Ronald Rhys all she wanted. He had always
been so odd, Abigail had no jealousy there.

She heard the trickle of water and knew she was close to the ravine. The deep path hit the dirt road again as her toes began to instinctively wrap around large rocks that led first to a small ditch and then a sudden cliff. It would have been easy to snake the road to the southwest a bit, and the bridge would have only had six or seven feet from the wood planks to the water underneath.

But the architect had been feeling romantic, and Abigail suspected they wanted the more breathtaking view, so instead, the bridge was built over the deepest part of the ravine where the sharpest and largest boulders displayed themselves, armed and ready for anything that might go over the edge.

Abigail didn't trust the bridge. During storms, pieces of it had been known to come right off and crash into splinters below. But she loved it just the same, and distrust never kept her from going to it or crossing it. She slipped her shoes back on, readjusted the potatoes on her shoulder, and crossed, determined to get this visit over with. Another fifteen minutes passed. The bridge was the second fork in the road. A fresh sign had been placed in front of her. Evie's pride and vanity were openly displayed right there on the road. To the right, a sign for MacGregor's Farms. Pointing left, a sign that read "Blackbriar Manor."

A manor? Really, Evie? Abigail rolled her eyes to the heavens and braced herself for what she would find at the end of the lane. Abigail was strong, as any baker would be after hauling sacks of flour from the grocer and kneading dough for hours every day, but by this time in her walk, the potatoes had become too much, and her hands ached. The muscles in her forearm twitched as she switched shoulders, and she rolled the free one back, trying to ease the pressure on her nerves. She was standing quite straight as she came to the clearing, not wanting Evie to see her struggling with the load.

Instead of remaining composed, however, she dropped the sack and gasped. What was before her eyes was beautiful and insane.

A circle drive presented an exquisite fountain, shooting water in dainty arches. The centerpiece of the fountain was a marble statue of a nude woman elegantly posed to draw your eyes from her jawline— framed and hidden by the length of her hair as she craned her neck behind her to see the front door—down to her nearly exposed breasts. They were just barely hidden by wire-framed peacock feathers, which were a work of art themselves. Inside each feather was an intricate mosaic of tiles and gemstones, glimmering turquoise and purple in the sun, blinding the viewer in such a way that it forced your eyes back to the statue behind them.

The face of the woman was turned to the front of the house, so as you walked the circle drive, you could not tear your eyes away from the smooth, white marble. Instead, they were searching, searching for the face. And there, as you reached the front steps, you found it, Evie's face smirking at you and your back to the front door.

The door opened, startling Abigail, and she spun around—exactly the effect Evie had intended—only to find Evie's sharp eyes staring down at her from the top of the steps. It was a disconcerting sensation of being surrounded by Evie.

"I see you met Esme." Evie gestured to the statue.

That statue would haunt her dreams, as would Evie's face that day on the steps. It would interlace over time with memories from a later date when Abigail would stand on the bridge she'd just crossed, looking down into the depths of the ravine. Hands grasping tight to the railing as she spotted the body laid out on the rock, blood swirling slowly into the water, until she made up her mind to walk away.

Abigail was silent as she approached the steps, which were also made of marble. She made her way to the mahogany-colored double doors.

Abigail found her voice. "I'm surprised you don't have hired help answering your door."

"Oh, don't be silly. It would spoil the effect. What do you have there? Oh, just come in."

The foyer was large, and a crystal chandelier hung from the vaulted ceiling. The right wall was mirrored from floor to ceiling, giving the open room to the left a disturbing grandness while reflecting, again, a second image of Evie's profile as she spoke.

"I don't know why our silly mother thinks she has to take care of me," she said. "The MacGregor boy brings me loads of produce."

"Why would he do that?" Abigail found herself asking.

Evie laughed. "Because he's in love with me, of course. That's the piano room," she said, waving her hand to the side as they continued deeper into the house.

"You don't play."

"So?"

Their mother would faint. Surely, the Rhys family didn't have this much money. Not after the war, anyway. "All this came from Ronald's trust fund?"

"Don't be silly."

They made their way to the kitchen, where Abigail was finally able to deposit the sack of potatoes. She ached all over.

"You need a bath, Abigail. Would you like to see mine?"

"Not particularly."

"Oh, you're no fun."

"Where is Ronald?"

"Wandering around drunk somewhere, I'm sure."

"It's barely noon."

"He bores easily." Evie lit a cigarette from a pack she pulled from some hidden fold of her dress. "Isn't it marvelous? I could run around naked like a heathen and no one would know. We could dance under the moon at midnight and expose our breasts to the stars! I love the woods."

"You hate the woods."

"Of course I do. But I do go skinny dipping in the fountain. It makes for a lovely wading pool." She blew the cigarette smoke out toward the ceiling. It swirled and then dissipated long before it could ever reach such great heights. "Come on, I hate kitchens."

The sisters continued to walk from room to room until they reached a half-finished ballroom and a stairwell that seemed to have been forgotten around eight feet. The expanse of woods behind the house was exposed, and Evie flicked her cigarette over a piece of hanging lumber.

"The workers won't come back until Ronald sells a few more paintings. And I've hired them all from out of town. I think this place shall be my grandest secret."

Abigail didn't believe for a second that Evie really wanted to keep it a secret. She just wanted it to seem that way. Surely, she expected Abigail to run into town and tell Jack and their mother, but she wouldn't give Evie the pleasure. "Ronald paints?" she asked, still searching the house for Evie's boy-groom.

"Oh, God no. While we were in New York, we found a man transporting art from Germany. The Nazis confiscated everything of value, and now that they are done, everything is just floating about." She waved her hand about as if the paintings just fell from the sky. "Lucky me, I met a man selling some very good pieces for cheap. Ronald bought them right away, and we're selling them to private collectors for ten times what we paid. You'd be amazed at what a bit of color on canvas goes for if it was slocked on by the right person."

"Evie, those items—they aren't . . ." Abigail didn't know what to say to her sister. "What about the families that art was taken from?"

"Well, they're probably all dead." She lit another cigarette. "You should really come back in a few months and see what I plan to do with the ballroom and the upstairs."

She wouldn't return until the day Evie died.

Part Three

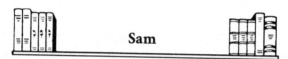

Sam

"Abigail—Ms. Lacey, um, Abigail." Sam held Abigail's hands in his, uncertain of how to talk to this woman. He'd known her his whole life—not well, but she'd always been around. It had been Abigail who had encouraged him to open a business. Abigail had introduced him to Everley Emmett, the man who owned the section of Main Street where Abigail's Bakery was perched and Sam's Deli would come to be stationed. Sam owed a good deal of his life's successes to this woman who always seemed to have the right idea and the right connection.

Yet he didn't really know her. He didn't know how to talk to her if they weren't discussing their businesses or AJ's venture across the street. Abigail always functioned, he realized, as an old, wise oracle of sorts. She was the one who told Sam that Sidney was back in town every time she was back in town. He had wondered if everyone had known how he felt about Sidney before they got together, if everyone had known that they had been together at AJ's wedding.

No, he knew now that it was just Abigail—Abigail, who somehow found out about everything and wanted the best for everyone. He supposed it was from years of having the Widows Club, as people liked to call it, meeting up at the bakery in the mornings for breakfast. Nancy Harrigan and her friends were a gossipy bunch. Now they ran a book club out of AJ's bookstore, so he supposed it would be AJ who would grow to know everything in time.

Abigail's hands were knotted and wrinkled in his. They must be sore from the arthritis. How was she still baking at all? He sent Hannah to help her as often as possible, but there were still days when Abigail would bake everything herself. Years of muscle memory and routine drowning out the pain and the forgetfulness of old age, he imagined. Abigail had run the bakery for so long that even on days she was sucked back to the 1950's, she was mostly able to keep going, making the same tarts she'd always made but handing them to customers who had long been dead.

"Old bird thought I was my father," Sam had heard people say.

Now, Sam tried again. "Abigail . . ."

"Just spit it out, Sam, before I lose my marbles."

He laughed. Abigail managed to be fully aware of her dementia after watching her mother suffer from it, and, when lucid, had quite a sense of humor about it, sometimes just moments after being belligerent and mean in her confusion.

He finally choked out the words. "I want to buy your house. We all want you to move in with Maude."

"I suppose that makes the best of sense, doesn't it?"

"Yes, it does," he said.

"And Maude will have me?"

"Why wouldn't she?"

Abigail nodded.

Sam continued, "Yes, she wants to move you into Jack's old writing room."

"I suppose that makes the best of sense, too. She wants Jack's desk and papers out of the house." Abigail pulled her hands from under his and placed them on top. "What will you do with my house, Sam?"

"Live in it."

"Why?"

"Because I love it. The timing is right."

"Good. A house needs to be loved. Buildings have history, you know. They're important. It can't just get run down by ill will."

"I agree."

"I'll let you buy my house, Sam. I'll move in with Maude, where I'll die knowing my house lives with someone who loves it."

Sam thought she sounded like she was talking about a cherished cat, not a house made of walls and beams and bricks. "Thank you, Abigail."

"It will cost you a pretty penny," she said, wagging her knotted knuckle at him.

"I'd expect nothing less."

"Let me call my real estate agent before I forget my name," she said. They both laughed even though neither one thought the situation was very funny at all. Sam even thought he saw a tear in the old woman's eye.

The paperwork took hours, as it tends to do when people are buying and selling houses. Abigail wasn't lucid for much of it, but her real estate agent had been called in time. All of Lily Hollow knew about Abigail's condition at this point, and Maude had already been given power of attorney.

It was not done quietly. Half the town was at the courthouse trying to nose their way into the meeting room. Everyone had a say in the matter, and many were upset that they weren't given the chance to bid on a much-coveted piece of property.

"This is a private sale. Go home!" Nancy Harrigan had materialized out of nowhere to help manage the scene.

Sam rubbed his eyes, exhilarated and terrified at the same time. He would soon own his own house. He was excited to be paying in full—decades of living with your mother and owning your own business has a way of beefing up your bank account. He was scared to death about all that money suddenly being gone, though. His whole life's work—all his savings—just gone along with the ink in his pen. He shook the pen to keep it from dying, but to no avail. His hand shook more. Abigail's real estate agent took it from his hand, tossed it in a nearby trashcan, and handed him a new one.

A thought struck him out of nowhere: Why did Abigail have a real-estate agent on retainer anyway?

"How long have you been Abigail's agent?" he asked the woman to his right.

"A little over a year. She called me and told me you'd be buying her house sometime and to just wait for her phone call and I'd make a nice commission. She wasn't going to sell to anyone but you while she was still alive. I have a notarized letter."

"And one last set of signatures," the man at the head of the table said, passing sheets around the table.

Sam took a deep breath. This was it. Sidney or no Sidney, it didn't matter. Sam was about to be a homeowner. Middle aged, and finally he was faced with the reality of adulthood.

"You ready?" one of the lawyers asked.

"Yep." Sam signed his name.

AJ and Matthew were behind Sam when he entered his house for the first time. The entryway was smaller than he remembered. The small end table covered in doilies would have to be removed, and that would open the place up a bit. Cobwebs that hung in the corners by the ceiling and the hardwood stairway that disappeared into the second floor needed to be swept.

"Has anyone cleaned this place?" Sam asked.

"Sidney did weeks ago, but I think she said she only got the kitchen and a bedroom," AJ answered. The heavy weight of Sidney's absence hit everyone.

The living room was small as well, but again, because outdated and oversized furniture was taking up most the space. The three made their way to the kitchen, which was adorable and immaculate. There were two downstairs bedrooms and a dining room with a window seat. Sam loved that dining room.

AJ had a box in her hand. "She'll want Granddaddy's books," she said, nodding to the china cabinet filled with books. Matthew took the box and started loading the books.

It took a few days to sort through it all and to talk to Abigail when she was able and find out what she wanted to take with her to Maude's. There wasn't much. It seemed everything "belonged to the house," which meant they were Lacey family heirlooms. She only took one suitcase of clothes and a handful of dresses and coats on hangers.

When Sam and Matthew moved furniture out of Jack Walters' old study, carrying the old oak desk to the Bookshop Hotel attic, Maude and AJ took turns sorting through belongings that would get moved into the room.

"It's all temporary," Abigail would say, waving her hand. "Stop fussing."

"Better now than later," Maude would reply.

It seemed to take longer than it actually did, mostly because everyone was wondering if Sidney was coming back. They were nearly done when she finally did.

Abigail

Abigail lay still in the bed of the guest room in the back of Maude's house. AJ had finally gotten Abigail to give up the tiny place she'd lived in for the last sixty-some-odd years. She'd held her hand, waltzed her out the front door of the dreary little bungalow, and said, "It's time you come home, Abby, to your family. Jack would have wanted it."

"Jack? Where is Jack?"

AJ patted her hand then like she patted her hand now. "How are you feeling today?"

Abigail was pretty lucid and shamefully aware of it. The awareness of the fact that sometimes you aren't very with it mentally is a sad state.

"Shouldn't you be at the Hotel, my dear?"

"Matthew's got it."

"How is that boy?"

AJ's smile was undeniable, a hint of a blush coming on. "He's good, really good."

AJ, so much like her great-grandfather when she actually smiled. She might have a Carson's complexion and coloring and her mother's face, but that smile was all Walters.

AJ sat down beside her bed with a box. "We found these hidden away in this room," AJ said, "with Granddaddy Jack's things."

"I see you met Esme," Abigail whispered, eyeing the box with suspicion.

AJ found it interesting that Abigail knew it by sight. How often had she seen Jack sneak things into what he supposed were hidden places? How much of their histories were locked away in this woman's memories?

Among photos and letters was a deed and a key. The deed was in Abigail's name but locked away in Jack's belongings. The key had been carefully placed on a lace ribbon but was tucked inside letters addressed to Jack. Most disturbing of all was a detailed sketch of a nude woman who looked a lot like Abby, draped in peacock feathers and dancing in water. It was from the hand of a talented, though obviously young, artist, and scrawled in the bottom corner was AJ's grandmother's name.

"Abby, what is all this from?"

"I own a castle in a forest," she said, feeling the drift of hazy sleep coming.

AJ smiled again. This time, it was an uncertain, tentative smile, the kind that came with a touch of sorrow and a bit of pity. That smile was just like Jack's, too. That smile was especially like Jack's. He'd had that exact smile the day he'd introduced Abigail to his new wife.

"Abby, Evelyn." Jack's hand had grabbed her arm, the familiar touch of childhood friends, his enthusiasm reminding her of his ten-year-old self leading her in a race through an open field. The tension had reminded her of all the times he'd caught her gaping at him like the schoolgirl she was. "Meet Emma Walters, my wife."

Abigail had stood there, stunned. Her sister, Evelyn, had put her hand out, long, slender fingers wrapping around both Emma's tiny little hands while she eyed Abigail meaningfully. "So lovely to meet you, Emma." Evie cruelly tilted Emma's left hand toward Abigail, flashing the ring into her line of vision.

"But Jack, you're only—"

"Nineteen. Who cares? A publisher picked up two of my books and wants more. The day I signed the contract, I asked Em here to marry me. We got married last week, and we're back in Lily Hollow to find a house. Isn't it wonderful?"

Abigail's world shattered in an instant. "Last week was my birthday," she said, forcing a smile. "What a lovely present." She gave Emma a quick, warm embrace. "Welcome to Lily Hollow. If you'll excuse me, I think I hear Mother calling."

Abigail left Jack standing there hand-in-hand with his new wife and Evie. God only knew what Evie was saying to the poor girl. Abigail passed the door to her own house and kept walking until she broke into a run. Of course, she had lied about her mother's voice, and halfway down Rose of Sharon Blvd., Abigail openly burst into tears.

Jack had gotten married the week she'd turned fifteen. She had been so certain that being fifteen would be the new beginning of everything and that by her sweet sixteen party one year from then, Jack would proudly escort her. She'd been in love with him her whole life. What better daydream than that?

Instead, he was married.

Instead of being giddy with his return, she was devastated.

Abigail cut through the woods and found her way to a grand road called Swan Lane. It was the road the construction crew was using to expand the school, so it was still dirt, but she assumed it would be paved soon. She ran until she found her way to MacGregor Bridge and sat there in Blackbriar Forest collecting herself for hours.

It was Evie who came to her, shockingly enough. She sat down next to her little sister, each hanging their feet over the edge, watching the water rush below. A good rain ensured it would be full and deep. A drought and the ditch would be nearly empty, a river run dry.

"I don't know why you came out here. My dress is getting dirty with just the idea of it."

Abigail didn't speak. She just watched her shoes as they swung back and forth on the tips of her toes. If they fell, she would lose them forever.

"I don't know why you're so upset," Evie continued. "If it wasn't going to be me, he was bound to bring someone home. He can't be alone. It just makes him grumpy."

Abigail gave her sister a look.

"All right, I know exactly why you're upset. But better he break her heart loving me forever than yours. You're my sister. She's no one."

Jack enlisted the moment he was able, though somewhat reluctantly. It was expected. It was the right thing to do. But he was scared. He watched his neighbors and friends leave and never come back. He'd seen how a man not coming home could change a whole family in the blink of an eye. He also saw how changed they were if they did make it back.

Ralph Carson lost an arm, and his brother Robert was gone forever. The only Carsons full bodied and alive were Abigail's age or younger. The Laceys had been hit pretty hard. Evie and Abby lost a father and a brother in the span of a month. With baby Jamie having died long before Abby's birth and another baby girl dead, the Laceys not only had no male heirs to carry on the name, but Mrs. Lacey had lost three children. Like many families, this war ensured that a lot of surnames died.

If Jack died at war before he was even able to marry and have children, the same would happen to "Walters."

During the war, after her father and brother died, Abigail spent countless hours with her uncle Ollie. Oliver Geoffrey Blythe was the twin brother of Oleander Gemma Lacey, Abigail's mother. He had been the first of Abigail's relatives to enlist and the only one to come home.

Soldier's heart, shell shock—the older people of Lily Hollow called it many things, but all Abigail could see was deep sadness and a steady fear of everything. Uncle Ollie mostly sat in a chair, staring at a painting that hung on the wall. It was a landscape he had done himself years before of a field Abigail knew to be a few miles down the road.

The wild roses had taken over, and people who visited Lily Hollow often said they'd never seen anything like it in all the world. In a town of gardeners, Abigail had always wondered what could possibly be so strange about it. There were extensive rose gardens all over town. Somewhere in history, someone had simply gotten carried away.

All of Lily Hollow was like that. Take a walk down Rose of Sharon Blvd. and you'd see the trees lined up in rows, usually in full bloom. Take a trip to the courthouse and cemetery and Easter lilies were in such abundance, the town organized lily digs where all the ladies brought decorated gardening buckets and pottery and transplanted them from the ground to send to the patients at the hospital in Briar.

During the war, the containers were all red, white, and blue. Stars and stripes were painted on them and sent to the soldiers. Abigail often baked sugarless tartlets to bundle up and send along as well. After Uncle Ollie came home, she made sure to keep some from every batch for him.

Ollie was thin and pale. Getting him to accept a blackberry tartlet was hard work, but once it was in his mouth, he savored and swallowed. The side of his mouth would twitch in what could only be considered an appreciative smile, though to call it a smile would be a serious stretch of the truth.

Where Abigail saw the war as an opportunity to be useful and help those who needed her, Evie saw all the dark sides of it and couldn't see past the harm it did. Evie didn't think anything they could do could possibly help anyone. She hated the war, and with that hatred, she cut out every reminder that it was happening.

She lived in a fantasy world where the war wasn't real and those who went off to fight in it were written off anyway, gone forever. She had no sympathy for Uncle Ollie. She claimed that her father and brother had abandoned the family, same as if they'd just walked off into the night, and Jack simply didn't exist at all.

While Jack was away, letters came to the house. Evie refused to read them, but Abigail couldn't leave them unopened. She wrote to him as often as they could afford the postage. Evelyn was stubborn and never once asked what was said in the letters. Only once did she show any sign of caring or even mention his name.

"You can tell Jack in that letter of yours that I plan to marry Ronald Rhys. He's half in love with me already. It won't take much." She shoved a bracelet onto her arm, an old piece of their mother's from the twenties that wasn't worth enough to bother selling when they were broke.

"Why would you say such a thing? Ronald Rhys is my age! You're too old for him!"

"But he's not a soldier."

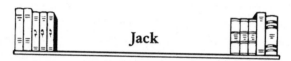

Jack

Abigail never visited Evie's estate again, not in her whole life, but she gave the key to Jack so he could.

It was after Maude was married. Henry Montgomery had taken her to the Hamptons. The Montgomerys had very little money, but Henry's father had a brother who did garden work for a family that did.

While the family was off vacationing in London, Henry's uncle had arranged a honeymoon adventure in the pool house.

Maude had only been gone a day when Jack grabbed Abigail's hand over their shared dinner. She was amazed that he was still capable of making her stomach do flip flops after all these years.

"Abby, I know you have the key."

"Excuse me?"

"The key. To the manor." Abigail pulled her hand away from his. She had never told him about the key or the lawyer who had called after Evie's death. Evelyn, for whatever reason, had left the manor, the estate, all the land to Abigail.

The lawyer had come to the house with a short note in Evie's handwriting and a large skeleton key, one that could only go to a large, ancient gate—or a vain woman's castle door in the woods.

To Abigail,

If I were you, I'd burn it to the ground and enjoy every last delicious flame. But you'll do something practical, I'm sure.
– E.

"To the manor," she'd written afterward as if Abigail were too dense to figure it out on her own. Abigail had burned the note, but she had neither done something practical nor burned down Evie's house. She had just left it. Abandoned.

Evie's fatal mistake when building the manor had been expecting gossip to take hold and send all the gawkers of Lily Hollow out to see it. The MacGregor boy had never spoken of it. His grocery delivery to the strange woman who'd bought his family's land was a stealthy secret. His mother would have been horrified to know that her son had anything to do, much less was enamored, with the woman in the woods. His father had been so upset at parting with more of his family's land, he wanted to hear nothing of the back twelve acres.

Abigail hadn't told anyone what her sister had done with the land she'd bought, simply because she knew that was what Evie had wanted. She had wanted Abigail to rave to their mother and for her mother to rant to her Sunday school friends and for those ladies to sneak out and have a peek for themselves.

In fact, Evie had been so certain that this was how it would pan out that she'd imagined it had actually happened, and so in a large grand house in the woods with everything, she'd spent most of her days staring out the windows of the upper floors like a hawk waiting to pounce on uneasy prey. When she'd never caught a glimpse of those supposedly sneaking glances, she'd chided herself for not having more trees removed during construction.

The police and the coroner who had come for Ronald Rhys when he'd shot himself were from Briar, the ghoulish estate having managed to fall into their jurisdiction rather than Lily Hollow's. And somehow, the folks of Briar hadn't seemed to care one lick about Evie, her house, or her antics.

And who would Jack have told? The daughter of the wife he had cheated on?

So instead, the house that time forgot had turned to ruins.

"I need the key, Abs," Jack repeated. "I just want to see it one last time. Put it all behind me."

It should have been put behind you ages ago, Abigail couldn't help thinking.

Abigail disappeared from her own dining room, leaving Jack to the dinner she had made him, and made her way to the upstairs. She'd hidden it in the furthest corner of the house, in the small room that had been converted from an attic to a nursery when she was too young to remember. The two tiny twin beds were still made up with flower-print comforters, and Abigail nearly bumped her head on the ceiling that sloped low enough for a child to pass unscathed but would leave an adult with quite a lump.

She sat on the bed—Evie's, as it was closest to the window—and lifted up the wooden panel that made the sill. Evie had a magnificent brain and heaps of talent that she had kept all to herself, too much of a snob to teach. If someone new ever bought the house, they would suspect the little hidey-hole created at the window was the work of a true carpenter.

But it was merely the work of a highly intelligent and sneaky child, hiding candies and stolen pocket money away while there was a depression on and the family could barely get by. As far as Abigail knew, Evie had never tried her hand at carpentry again, never having a good enough reason to bother.

Abigail peeked inside. Little bits and scraps that had remained after Evie left the house and then the object Jack wanted—the key, dropped there to be forgotten along with everything else of Evie's, the house, and that ghastly fountain.

Jack

Jack held the key in his hand. Only Evie would have made a point to have something made for her new mansion that looked so old and dated. Years later, it looked like the real deal, an ancient key to some-place gothic and magical. Holding it in his hand, he remembered passing her a copy of *Jane Eyre*, begging her to read it, thinking she'd adore the sheer oldness of it. Instead, she'd brought it back to him and said, "What a prude. I hate Jane Eyre."

Abigail, not far behind, had piped up, "Jack, I think Jane was wonderful."

Of course Abigail would. The kid was so starved for love from her sister, she latched on to anyone of that age for that affection. She would have liked anything Jack liked, always seeking his approval. He remembered patting her head and saying, "Well, you have great taste in literature," even though he knew she didn't really care about the book at all, just him.

He'd tried so hard to share his own family's love for books with the Laceys, but they'd never caught on. The girls' mother, Mrs. Oleander Gemma Lacey—Jack loved saying her whole name—had been far too intent on the girls learning to work hard and not be idle to give them another excuse to drift off into their heads. Evelyn had always been taken with the sheer joy of doing nothing, and Abigail had been inclined to forget chores mid-cartwheel in the grass.

Abigail hadn't actually been forgetful. She'd just been a kid. Everyone had known she'd fall in line with her mother's wishes, have strong work ethic, and be a good person. But Evie would never conform. Evie had seen the world as an egg that needed to be cracked and poured out over a hot skillet so she could watch it sizzle and squirm. What little schoolwork and reading she'd bothered to do, she'd misconstrued or twisted simply for the pleasure.

Jack had hoped to find his way in through books. Her family had been ambivalent to books, so maybe she would choose to go against the grain and cherish them with him. But that wasn't how Evie worked. The second you thought you had her pinned down, she'd do something completely different on you.

When Evie rejected *Jane Eyre*, somehow Jack knew he had lost and would continue to lose. Being friends with Evie was quite possibly the loneliest life he could pursue. Evie didn't have friends, only people who wanted her approval or company for some reason or another. And for some reason, Evie had liked it that way.

Jack looked away from the key in the palm of his hand to Abigail. She offered him a meek, half-hearted smile. It pained him sometimes that she loved him so unconditionally, was so devoted, so helpful, was everything a wife should be. His eyes darted away from her to the china cabinet behind her. Except it wasn't filled with china. Instead, it was peppered with some books he remembered recommending to Evie, along with his own life's work to date.

"Were those Evie's? I thought you didn't keep anything of hers."

"I didn't. Those are mine."

Of course. He nodded quietly, tapping the key against his hand.

"Jack."

"Yes?"

"Just go."

He'd driven out here many times over the years, mostly just to sit at the bridge. The letter had haunted him for so long. She had expected him to come, he knew that. She had expected him to see her in her last moments, to say goodbye, to make some kind of visual impact on him for life. She wanted him to see her death, had made notes about it in the scraps of letters she'd mailed him before she died. But he hadn't. Instead, she'd died all alone. She had imagined their connection so strong that he would just know to come. And somehow, he had known, but he was too late.

If Maude hadn't peed her pants right as he had decided to leave the house, right in the doorway . . . "I peed. Sawwee." If he had known anything about anything—how to make the child stop crying when he was frustrated, too, where Emma and Abigail had kept her extra bloomers that matched all her dresses—then maybe he wouldn't have been so worked up and frustrated over the accident and unable to find anything.

Why wasn't Abigail at the bakery that morning when he needed to feed Maude and saw that he hadn't bought groceries since the funeral and all the food from the church people had finally run out or gone bad? Later, she would tell him she'd forgotten to open, but that was a lie. Abigail, of all people, never lied to him, so the one time she did, it was so boldfaced and badly done, he was too baffled to call her on it and too tired to try to figure it out.

Everything had just suddenly become too much for him, and to end up at the grocery store with a child crying in hunger while trying to determine what on earth was best to feed her and then to hear that Ronald Rhys had killed himself . . . He bought a bunch of bananas and rushed home to sit there and watch his daughter devour two and a glass of milk before whisking her out the door, only to have her stop on the threshold in panic as a puddle appeared between her legs below. "Sawwee, Daddy. I peed," she repeated when he didn't move right away.

"Oh, Maude," he said, ushering her back into the house so he could find towels and new clothes. Evie was out there on that estate all alone, and he was here cleaning pee. Later, he'd realize that Evie was out there bleeding out on a rock while he was hunched over his threshold cleaning pee, he thought now as the car rumbled over the bridge. He didn't have to look out the window at the rocks and the water below. He had them memorized by heart.

The gravel from the road started to crunch as soon as the vehicle rolled off the end of the bridge, gravel Evie had put out there, tired of all the dirt. She never spoke to him after that day in the woods during the war, but he knew her and had known her mind. He knew what she would say, had she been speaking. He knew what she was thinking—at least, he always thought he did. He knew her distaste for things getting her dirty and knew she liked things that looked shiny and new. Once, this gravel had sparkled white, hiding the dirt. Now it was old, unkempt, and mostly dirt itself.

He took the left at the fork, the Blackbriar Manor sign long gone missing, but he knew the way. Then, there they were, the black cast-iron gates, smashed open by something or another, and the fountain. The white marble statue was smeared green with moss and mold. Green moss had worked its way through the fountain, left full of murky pond water and minnows. Frogs had taken over the place, and he could hear them leaping and darting about when he got out of the car to walk the circle drive. It was worth the walk—always had been—to trace your steps around such a beautiful piece of art in search of the best face you would ever know.

But now, as he got to the face, he saw that it was not that beautiful, and the eyes were menacing. He stared and stared into the soulless figure and imagined he heard the door open behind him, imagined the presence in the doorway, imagined that sensation of being surrounded by Evie. And in that moment, he realized he didn't love her at all. He hated her. He hated her more than he could have ever loved her.

She was horrible, he realized. She was completely and utterly horrible. The knowledge of his life so wasted fantasizing his passion for this. And Emma, getting the raw end of the deal, being politely idolized but never properly cherished. Then Abigail. He shook his head and saw the statue and Evie and Abigail all for what they really were and turned to use the key on the door.

He hadn't actually needed the key, he noticed, as the door creaked open, the hinges half rotted away. Evie had commissioned a castle to be built, but the house had not been built well, only quickly with lots of shine to it. The mirrors in the entryway had long ago been smashed. Perhaps a teenager or two had come by and chosen to vandalize the place, knowing no one would know.

The floors, once so extravagant, weren't much more than additional forest floor, mud smeared across the marble floors, weeds coming up where the soil had been more thickly clumped. A family of raccoons was living under and in the piano, the piano room all dark and musty. As Jack stepped into the main room, though, he was met with sunshine. A tree had fallen through the roof of the vaulted ceiling.

This place was like Evie—pretty at first, but given to uselessness, rotting from the inside out. It depressed him, and instead of spending hours lurking about and searching for any remains of a life that was gone, he ran within moments. He got in his car and drove down the gravel, to the fork, across the bridge, and back into town. He drove until his heart was beating fast and he came to a screeching halt in front of the hotel.

He had been sitting in the gardens for hours when Abigail arrived.

"How did you know I was here?"

"Because I gave you the key." She held her hand out for it.

"I left it in the door."

"Even better." She set her hands on her knees.

"But didn't you think I'd be there? At the manor?"

"No, Jack. That place is depressing and awful. It was then, and I'm sure since I left it to its own devices, it would be even worse."

"I'm going to have to shut this place up like that. We're just not making the money any more. I keep holding on, and I want to pass it to Maude, but I just don't think we can keep our doors open but a few more years."

"But this . . ." She looked around at the hotel walls. "This is just the opposite. Even when we lock its doors, it won't fall apart. It won't crumple. This place was built with love. It's sturdy. This hotel will always make it. The manor just wasn't—just isn't."

Sidney

In Briar, Sidney slid into a booth at the coffee shop in the town square. She'd been coming for a few days now; it was within walking distance of the bed and breakfast she'd checked into after the last fight with Sam. The lattes were as good as Matthew's, the regular coffee pretty standard. They carried a wide assortment of teas and also served alcohol in the evenings. It looked as though years ago it may have been more of an ice cream or soda shop, based on the designs of the booths. The colors were all subdued like a coffeehouse or pub, but the infrastructure seemed similar to Sam's.

The place was cozy, and Sidney was surprised she hadn't visited or even heard of the place before renting the room at the bed and breakfast over the last week. It had clearly been around a while, and like Abigail's was for Lily Hollow, it seemed to be a Briar staple. There were always a handful of people peppered along the bar stools, someone in a booth, and to-go orders going out the door. In the evenings, there was standing room only if she walked in after sundown.

A hunched old man sat opposite her one booth over. He was here often and usually had a cup of tea and read a newspaper. Despite it being late in the morning, he looked tired, as though he had just woken up. Normally, Sidney would have dismissed this man.

She had a habit of sifting through crowds with a needs-based eye. "What can they do for me?" Often, if it wasn't a young, attractive male, her eyes darted to the next person. After so much time helping at the bookstore and caring for Abigail, she saw him differently than she would have just a year ago. Just because someone was old didn't mean they had nothing to offer; and even if someone had nothing to offer, it didn't mean there wasn't something you could offer them.

The barista brought her a latte and a fresh cup of tea for the old man. "Here, Granddad," she said. Ah, he was probably the owner.

"This is a neat place," Sidney said after the girl left. "Are you the owner?"

"Yes and no," he said. "It was my wife's. We agreed to pass it to the children. I'm more of a dedicated patron."

Sidney smiled. He had a nice voice and a slight accent. His hands shook a bit as he dropped a sugar cube into his cup. Sidney liked that there were no sugar packets to be seen, only jars of sugar cubes. AJ would love this place, and Sidney wondered if she had ever been. Sam would like it, too. And Abigail. Not Maude, though. Maude didn't care for being somewhere she couldn't be useful and clean. Not very relaxed, her mother.

This place made you feel at home. It made you think of your family. There were family portraits along the wall, and Sidney caught herself searching for the man in tweed on the walls. She spotted him quickly. The old man across from her had been handsome.

"My wife's family," he commented.

"I see that. Your family, too."

"Mostly. My children, of course. There's a few important members missing, but I suppose they don't belong on the walls here."

Sidney nodded, pretending to know what he meant, but she was at a loss. She'd noticed with Abigail how much the elderly seemed to prattle. There was meaning in everything they said, but much of that meaning was lost to time and life experiences the young hadn't had yet.

"Like who?" she asked.

"Oh, my parents, of course. They died in England. I never saw them again after I came here. Friends, lovers. People who impact your life most are family in a sense. Doesn't mean they're welcomed in family portraits, but they are not meant to be forgotten, either."

Sidney understood that. She thought of Jude. If he'd been kinder, more responsible, stayed in touch, would they have taken family portraits? She knew people who'd had children together but weren't together who managed to be civil like that. Civility and pointedly ignoring someone were not the same thing.

It didn't matter how many years she went without seeing him or wanting to see him. Jude still had a piece of her and always would. She couldn't forget him, couldn't forget the lessons she'd learned from experiencing the cruelty of being dismissed. Her whole life had been different because she'd known him, but they were nothing to each other.

"You want to know when to include them and when not to," he said.

Her eyebrows went up. It wasn't a question. It was a statement. Yes. How did he know? She wanted to know so badly! Jude was left to the past, and she didn't know if one day she'd see Sam in the same light, a person you thought your whole world revolved around, who would change the course of your universe, but who ultimately needed to be cast aside to a memory box for your own self-preservation. For their preservation.

He licked his thumb and turned the page of his paper as though he'd been reading the whole time they were talking. Then he leaned forward on his tweed forearms and looked at her hard. He patted the table across from him, and Sidney picked up her things and moved closer, now sharing his booth. She leaned across the table, too, and looked closely into the old man's watery eyes. They were deep wells, eyes that had seen much and felt everything deeply and stored it all away like stolen treasure.

"I lived a happy life. I loved my wife and our children. Still do, even though she's gone. I miss her. Sometimes, though, when I get to thinking, I miss the people not in those photos more."

"Because you didn't get as much time with them?"

"Perhaps. Mostly because they knew me best. Kept my secrets."

"How long were you married?"

"Longer than you've lived."

"And she didn't know you best?"

"She knew what I became, but not all that I ever was." He stirred his tea, needing to do something with his shaky hands.

"Do you regret marrying her?"

"Never."

Sidney thought on this. To want to have done things differently and yet not regret the outcome of what you did. To want a life with Sam even though she wished she could have offered AJ a traditional home. When she looked back as an old, old woman, what would Sam be? Family? Just an ex-lover? A mistake? Someone missing from photographs? A husband? A secret-keeper?

"What would have been ideal?" Sidney asked the man.

"Oh, I can't answer that." He sipped his tea. "What makes a woman like yourself so unsure?"

"Unsure of what?"

"Of a man's love for you."

"It's not that. I don't know if I know how to love him enough back. I'm always in relationships, but I like being on my own. I suppose I could be happy anywhere with anyone, but I could be miserable anywhere with anyone, too. I'm a little prone to misery, and I bring it out in people."

"You Lily Hollow women are all alike." He said it warmly with a smile and picked up his paper. At the door to the coffee shop was a cane. He took it and unsteadily walked out and down the sidewalk.

"Granddad likes his walks," the barista said.

Sidney realized she must have looked perplexed. She paid her bill, left a tip, and hurried out the door, but the man had gone.

Peter

Peter had begun carrying a walking stick. After meeting Abigail, he found that his hands were fidgety on the days she didn't pop up on his trails, which were twenty-nine out of thirty. Without that hand hooked into the crook of his arm, the arm became restless and needed to wing about a bit. The stick let him lash out at the brush like a boy—Peter Pan the swordsman instead of Peter Pendritch the school teacher.

He'd been walking with Abigail for a little over a year now, but that meant he'd only actually seen her about fourteen times. He felt as though he knew her pretty well, despite the infrequency, and the more he saw her, the more he missed her the rest of the month. About six months ago, they had exchanged telephone numbers, and they spoke on the phone once a week, which helped, but neither one was very chatty unless face to face, and the calls were generally an awkward five minutes of checking in on each other and discussing the weather before they hung up.

He looked up at the sky and checked his pocket watch. What did she think about on these long treks to see him every month? He rushed away from the high school as quickly as possible on the days he knew she'd come. It was the only day of the month he didn't offer tutoring.

He made it to the hollowed-out tree, where he squirreled away his walking stick so his arm would be free for her, and kept his pace toward Lily Hollow. Then he heard her footfalls on the path ahead and felt his own heart skip a beat. He saw her face start to materialize among the tree leaves, her cheeks rosy from the exercise, her eyes with smile lines around them, and her whole face beaming, drawing him closer.

"Peter!" she said, slightly out of breath. "I think I ran nearly half-way here. I got such a late start."

"Eager to see me?"

"Always." Their arms met, and they grasped each other so that each had a hand tight across the other's forearm as they stumbled into a steady hug. She kissed his cheek before pulling away.

She rubbed her lips together. "You're quite the prickly pear today. Growing a beard?"

He rubbed his jaw. "Perhaps."

"Hmmm."

"Do you like bearded men?" He raised his eyebrows at her, and she stood back a minute, pretending to survey him but secretly admiring him.

Peter Pendritch was a scholarly handsome. His eyebrows were a tad too bushy, he wore glasses, and his hair was often wild and unkempt, but he looked exactly how a mad-scientist-turned-literature-teacher who longed to live in the trees like the Swiss Family Robinson should look, only handsomer.

She always thought his eyes would look lovely on a little girl. His nose was strong. She couldn't help but plaster his face with kisses when she saw him. His walking kept him leaner than his frame might have naturally been. When the weather was warmer, like today, he often left his coats behind, and she could see his muscles through his dress shirts—the muscle of a man who walked every day, scrambled over rocks often, and did yard work on Saturdays.

She imagined if he ever had to rearrange his classroom, he could lift the school desks over his head with ease. Seeing how the young boys at her church who were playing football and on the wrestling team lifted weights, she appreciated more and more the practical muscle of her generation.

They took a path Abigail hadn't been down before, but she trusted Peter implicitly and followed him without hesitation. It dead-ended in a clearing of daisies.

"Oh, Peter, can we sit a minute? It's so lovely."

"I thought you might want to."

Of course, Abigail wasn't one for politely sitting in the woods, and she threw herself with utter abandon on the blanket of white and yellow petals, staring into the sky.

"It's been a long month, Peter."

"For me, too." He lay down next to her, only inches apart. "Maybe you could start taking an extra day off and come out twice a month." He raised his eyebrows at her conspiratorially so that she laughed. He loved her laugh. He loved making her laugh.

"Oh sure, throw all caution to the wind."

"Yes, why not?" He took her hand, and she let him.

She turned her head to face him, and their noses nearly touched. He could smell lemon meringue on her breath, and his fingers tightened around hers.

"I like my life exactly the way it is," she said.

He could see every eyelash, every pore in her skin. Just one more inch and his mouth could be on hers, but he sensed her holding back, so he did, too.

"You don't want more?"

"More of what? This is perfect." She let go of his hand and threw her arms behind her head like a boy. After a few minutes, he sat up and looked her up and down, lying there with daisies tickling her arms and waist . . . her blouse having come untucked a bit from the band of her slacks . . . just the tiniest square inch of creamy flesh exposed, kissed by the flower petal on her left, just above the hip, right below the rib. His hand only inches away from it in the grass. He lifted his hand up to scoop his hair out of his face and purposely brushed past her skin just so.

"That tickled," she whispered. "I should go!" she said louder and bolted upright just as he leaned forward. But in doing so, their heads knocked together, and they began laughing so hard, his eyes actually began to tear up.

"Oh, Peter! I've broken you!" She laughed, holding his cheeks in her hands. "Are you okay?"

"I'm fine," he laughed. "Just going to have a good egg on my forehead."

She kissed his head, then his cheek. Then he kissed her right on the lips.

She was frigid at first, startled and confused, until she let go and allowed him to kiss her properly.

"Peter," she said, pulling his face away, still cupped in her hands, "I really must go."

"What have you got to do?"

"Truly? Absolutely nothing."

"Then why should you go?"

"Because I'd rather walk home than have you drive me."

"I don't mind the drive."

"It's not the point."

"I love you," he blurted.

"That's not the point, either." And she disappeared down the trail the same way they'd come.

He lay back in the grass, where their imprints remained like snow angels, and pressed his hand where hers had been.

The reserved woman he had met just a year ago had grown into a girlish free spirit. She'd gone from a timid thing, always worried about some responsibility or another, to a sprite, carefree and sure of herself. He had imagined it had been he who had drawn it out of her, proudly taking responsibility for her good humor. But now he knew he'd been wrong. He'd been so very wrong.

These woods! Abigail spread her arms wide as she walked, touching the leaves of the trees with her fingertips. A few times, a tree branch hung low, close to her face. Instead of ducking below it or brushing it aside with her hand, she found herself stopping to stare at it—all of its tiny parts, all of its flaws, all of its leafy green texture. Before she could stop herself, she licked it, then found herself in a fit of giggles like a ten-year-old.

These woods were her life's blood. What would she do without her walks? She didn't know.

It was hours before she was expected home again, and she could have spent hours more with Peter, that beautiful man. But it was the freedom of the woods she craved on these days off, not beautiful, perfect, darling Peter.

She let her mind wander to him and what a life with Peter would look like. He had a house on the edge of Briar, where the backyard butted against these very woods. There was a gate in his back garden leading to them. He had rows and rows of radishes, their purple blooms popping up a few inches above the earth. She could see herself happy there, maybe the longed-for baby or two on her hip in a few years. She knew he wanted children.

She imagined she would have to close the bakery or hire someone to actually do the baking a few times a week. She shook her head. She wouldn't have to, but if there were children at home, she would want to. Abigail had found the stride in life where one knows oneself and, faced with any decision, knows exactly what she would do with it. Not wisdom, really. Just a self-awareness that comes about from grief and trial and the recovery of the whimsy of childhood.

She imagined discussing Peter's students with him over dinner and even helping him with his experiments in the basement after their children were asleep, tucked snugly in their beds. A boy and two girls, she could see them clear as day. And she loved them, she loved them all, especially Peter, who was real.

But for no particular reason at all, she just didn't want them. She didn't want to close the bakery, nor did she want to try to do both. She didn't want to leave her home in Lily Hollow, nor did she want to uproot him and have him join her. She wanted it all to stay as it was. She wanted the woods to herself for a time, the companionship of Peter now and then, and then to go back home and enjoy what she had built over the years. She loved her bakery. She loved her aging mother. She loved Jack and Maude in a way she hadn't imagined possible for a woman who was neither a wife nor a mother to them.

Abigail emerged from the woods and found that she'd wandered by way of the hotel. Jack was behind the gardens, staring off into space, and as a result was facing her when she hit the pebbled walkway.

"You look fantastic," he said. She imagined she did or he wouldn't have said it. Jack wasn't one for just blurting out observations unless he felt shockingly passionate about them and truly meant them. She brushed a bit of grass out of her hair and smiled at him.

"I know," she said, continuing on her way.

The corner of Jack's mouth twitched a bit as Evie came to mind. He had to admit to himself it had been some time since she'd sneaked up on him like that.

He spun around. "Abigail!" he called after her.

She waived her hand overhead and hollered back at him. "Not now, Jack! I'm having a good day!"

It's that feeling of close but not there yet, the tension created in the space between two bodies. The sensation of a presence without the texture of touch to accompany it. When the hair rises up on the skin in a desperate attempt to bridge the gap between your space and their space, causing tiny little bits to reach out with it . . . goosebumps.

Then when they retreat back into your skin, it's as though they continue to flee as far as they can, running from the hint of rejection, diving into the pit of your stomach where they'll bounce around in confusion as butterflies.

They jumble up and cause chaos within. The heart races, and the breath tries desperately not to become a gasp until, finally, you realize the dreadful, exciting, beautiful experience has started all over again. Finally, the body is relieved from that stress by a simple moment of . . . contact.

That's what it was like for Peter every time he saw Abigail. The sensations began every time he even thought about seeing her.

So that must be love, right?

His parents had been writing him incessantly about it being due time to bring a wife back to England. Why was he still in America? What did he plan to do with the rest of his life? When would they see their bloody grandchildren?

He had always been more in love with science than the people around him, more in love with literature than in love, which wasn't saying much. And more than anything, he adored his walks, the time alone to gather his thoughts and really think about the world and his place in it. Then Abigail came crashing through and inserted herself into his alone time and, in doing so, made him realize that he enjoyed sharing that time with someone.

The sun was going down, and his encounter with Abigail in the woods was long over as he stepped into the town square of Briar. He breathed the town in and made note of the differences between the air here and that of the woods. He took in the smell of the cars, the pavement, and even the cobblestone when he hit Market Street.

The mood lighting of the café always called to him. He liked the way the street light glinted off the window and blinded him from what he knew was within. Peer a bit closer and you could see past the light to the twinkling of lamps and garden lights hanging from the ceiling. There was no place like it.

"No Abigail today?" the girl behind the counter asked.

"Mmm?"

"Abigail Lacey from Lily Hollow. Usually comes with you this time of the month."

"Oh yes, she does. No, not today. Maybe not ever again. I don't suppose I know."

Jack

Jack held a pen in his writing hand and tapped his notebook. He'd been at the process for far too long to change his routine. Computers had never made their way into his life, and he wrote everything by hand before typing it on the typewriter.

Dozens of titles and he still wondered if he'd ever write anything any good. How many people had read his novels and even praised them? But they still didn't hold a candle to his own literary tastes. He'd wanted to write something amazing. If he'd been able to capture even a fraction of what he'd felt and lived on paper, he'd have been satisfied, but he never got it quite right.

He tapped the pen on the paper again. Maude was folded up in a chair with a sketchbook, probably drawing him. His grown and lonely daughter, husbandless and with a small child in the other room. Seemed the Walters were destined to raise children alone.

But not alone, he reminded himself. They always had Abigail, he thought as his lifelong friend stepped out onto the back porch with baby Sidney on her hip.

"Working on a new one, Jack?" she asked.

He smiled and nodded a bit. He looked down at his paper. He'd written Evie's name out in a doodle, not thinking, not paying attention. An old habit from starting letters to her that would never be sent and speaking to her in his journals.

He scratched it out somewhat viciously and caught a look from Abigail out of the corner of his eye.

Abigail. She deserved a story, not Evie. But what to say about Abigail always evaded him. Where Evie was every love interest, every temptress, every villain, Abigail had always simply managed to be Abigail.

Maude stood at the kitchen window with her daughter. Their elbows touched slightly as Maude scrubbed the dinner dishes and Sidney dried, despite Maude's height. Little AJ was in the living room reading a book. Well, not so little anymore. She was twelve now and completely uncertain of what to say around her mysterious mother who had arrived at their home the week before for a visit. AJ spent most of the visit watching Sidney when she thought no one was paying attention and hiding in a book when she thought someone was. It was warm in the kitchen, and Maude wiped sweat from her brow with her soapy left hand.

"Thank you for dinner, Maude," Sidney said. Maude felt her brow furrow. Even though she couldn't remember the last time Sidney had called her "Mom" or "Mama," it stabbed her in the heart every time she called her by name. What kind of mother was she to not even earn the title?

She'd always thought she would offer her child more than her father had offered her, but she seemed incapable of the warmth and tenderheartedness she saw in other mothers. She felt those things for her daughter. She just didn't know how to show it, and her lack of proper mothering was proven repeatedly by Sidney's actions—first by Sidney's inability to call her "Mom," then by getting pregnant out of wedlock in high school, and now in the way she acted toward AJ.

Maude plunged her hands into the sink and drew out another plate. Her hands had aged right before her eyes, years of burning fingers on stovetops cooking for her family, of doing dishes, of gripping pencils when she drew . . . Years of life just etched across her hands. Her hands looked three times as old as she felt, and she didn't feel young.

"What do you think they're talking about?" Sidney asked, nodding to Abigail and Jack in the backyard.

The two were huddled together on the garden bench, looking out over a mass of roses and tomatoes. Abigail's hand was cupped over Jack's.

Jack leaned in to Abigail and said something, and Maude dropped her gaze down to the bubbles in the sink. It didn't matter that she couldn't hear them. Maude felt like seeing them have a private conversation was as good as eavesdropping, and she'd learned long ago not to do that.

She looked back up, though, her curiosity always getting the better of her even now as an adult. Not just an adult, a grandmother. She enjoyed watching the two of them together, always had. *Abigail would have made a lovely mother*, she caught herself thinking, and not for the first time.

It was Abigail who taught her how to be a grandmother to AJ. It was Abigail who taught her how to fill someone else's shoes the best she could when that someone else left someone in need of a mother, without demanding the title of motherhood. She started to turn to glance at AJ. The girl was perched in the living room pretending not to be bothered by things like abandonment and being raised by old people. But a movement at the window caught Maude's eye again.

Jack had pulled his hand away from Abigail's with a jerk, and Abigail stood. Maude watched the old woman head to the back gate and leave with tears pouring down her face. Jack's face was pruned up in an expression Maude knew well but hadn't seen since Sidney was a tiny little thing. He was upset—very upset.

"What was that?" Sidney asked, dropping the towel, ready to charge the door.

Maude grabbed her daughter's arm. "Abigail always was a bit in love with Daddy," she said quietly. "I imagine it had something to do with that. Let him be."

"Who is in love with whom?" AJ marched into the kitchen to pull lemonade from the fridge and fill her empty glass.

"Apparently, Abigail has been in love with Granddaddy all this time."

AJ nodded. "That makes sense."

"It's good to have Sidney back for a bit," Jack had sighed. He had leaned back into the old bench and settled in for a chat. Abigail liked their chats these days as much as she enjoyed her walks in the woods. Jack was calm and good natured lately. He had taken the role of grandfather well, and being a great-grandfather was sheer bliss. "All my girls in the same house again. Sometimes, I wonder if I did right sending her away like that."

Abigail nodded to Jack. He was prattling away. He didn't chatter often, but when he was happy—especially after a good meal—he let out things that normally stayed bottled up.

"You did the best you could, Jack," Abigail said and put her hand over his.

"Still, there's things I regret." He accepted the hand pat, then caught her thumb with his, trapping her hand from pulling away. Abigail gave in and left her hand on his a moment longer.

"We're old, Jack. We'd be unwise to not think of something regretful. If we regretted nothing, we'd have nothing to learn from. There are always mistakes. That's okay. You've done well learning from yours over the years."

"You've done well teaching me how."

Abigail smiled at him sheepishly. Her hand tingled a bit where his thumb was resting. A girlish sensation left over from years of loving someone so much? Maybe. Probably just losing feeling where her arthritis liked to set in. "You give me too much credit," she said.

"Abby, we should have done it long ago . . ."

Abigail raised her eyebrows.

"Married, Abby. I'd like to get married. I owe you that."

Abigail's breath caught in her throat.

"Well?" he asked expectantly, as though she would surely jump at the opportunity.

Abigail's mind rushed. Years ago, that was all she wanted. Years ago. Then she wouldn't have done so even if her life depended on it. He was having such a terrible time, he'd been a downright "horse's arse," as Peter would have said. Now . . . Well, what now? Was this some consolation prize he was offering up to her because she was the one still standing, still loving him?

Besides, they had a lovely life now. Her friendship with him was something to be cherished, and truth be told, she was still madly in love with him and always would be. After all these years, could she suddenly become a wife? Would she even know how? Did she even want to? Looking into his face, hearing that question now at their age, she knew the answer, and she shook her head no.

"No, no, Jack . . ."

"But we love each other. We could spend what we have left together."

"We'll do that anyway."

"But Abby . . ."

"Jack, you don't mean it."

"I do, Abby," he said earnestly. "I do."

"No."

Jack jerked his hand from hers. "I don't understand you," he said. He sounded angry.

"I understand you too well, my love."

She stood and headed to the gate. She couldn't let him see her cry. He would take it as a sign of remorse, as though there was a chink in her armor, a chance to ask again. She couldn't let him think she would change her mind or to presume she misspoke in haste.

She cried all the way home.

George

George straightened his tie. His father had liked bow ties, which George, of course, had always found old-fashioned and silly. Straightening his tie around his collar now, he wished he hadn't been so rude to his father about them. He'd been so pretentious. He looked pretentious now. He ripped the silk tie from his throat and decided not to wear anything around his neck at all. The lawyer be damned.

No, he needed the lawyer. He needed the lawyer to fight this sale. He needed to do everything they asked. Act how they said to act, be who they wanted him to be. They told him to wear a tie. Just a tie, not his usual high-dollar suits that made him seem greedy and intense. That bookstore lady and the judge needed to sympathize with a man cut out of his inheritance, his legacy, they said.

That's it. He'd wear one of his father's bow ties. They were in the other room, all paisleys, all ridiculous. But when he went to fetch one, seeing them in the drawer made him feel close to his father. Wearing one made him feel like his father's son again.

George realized that since his father's death, after dealing with funeral homes and lawyers and people who needed to know he had some sort of official claim on the man, that he had begun to think of George, Sr. as "Father" instead of "Dad." While he'd been alive, he'd only ever called him "Dad"—"Daddy" when he was very small. He hungrily held all the ties close to his chest. He needed these. He needed his father. He needed them all. Needed his dad. He needed the books back, too. He wanted them. He wanted everything his father had ever touched and he wanted it in front of him now. He wanted . . .

He started to sob uncontrollably like a child.

He wanted his daddy.

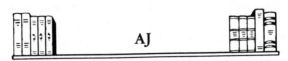

AJ

AJ strained to see what was actually in the letters sent by certified mail by the lawyers. They looked like duplicates, ten copies of the same thing, but she was so tired, she couldn't be sure that her mind wasn't betraying her somehow. No longer able to decode the written language, her head pounded from the stress.

Just a few short months ago, everything had been easy, and she had taken it for granted. The Bookshop Hotel had come into being almost as though it had always existed. Not that she and Matthew hadn't put in hours of sweat and hard work, but their hard work had always gotten them the result they'd desired. Who lives with such gratification? No one. She'd been living a dream, and now the dream was falling apart.

Abigail was not long for this world, stumbling in and out of realities AJ not only didn't understand but didn't *want* to understand. The tidbits she had put together only seemed to reveal that Granddaddy Jack might not have always been the amazing and trustworthy man she had loved so well her whole life. What was important was that he had become that man. Did she really want to know all the dirty secrets that had led him to that point? Was that necessary? Or could she just enjoy the memories she wanted?

Now, this George Edelstein business . . . Did this trial have to happen now? Now, when Abigail was so sick, when Sam and Sidney's volatile relationship had the whole town on an emotional rollercoaster? Now, when this gala was supposed to be the talk of the season?

She supposed it would be the talk of the season anyway, regardless of how much limelight Sidney and Sam might suck out of the affair and regardless of whatever Abigail would be lucid enough to enjoy. George Edelstein would ensure it was the talk of the season when everyone arrived to see nothing.

No rare and antiquarian reading room. No world-class collection that seasoned collectors would treat as a destination vacation. Nothing.

It had all been too easy, of course, and now it was all slipping away.

At the moment, there was nothing she could do but wait. Her hands itched to be productive, but she couldn't work on the project that had consumed every waking thought for the last few months. She supposed cleaning would work or even rearranging the main display table in the entrance. But it all turned her stomach, because she knew she'd just be thinking of her efforts being noticed at the gala.

Matthew came into the office with a mug full of something foamy and caffeinated. A hint of lavender hit her nose. He'd been experimenting with various tea lattes lately, but this still managed to be a cappuccino of sorts. She barely glanced at it.

He rested his hand on her shoulders. When things were good, she would have graciously accepted this concoction and perhaps cupped her hand over his. Instead, she shrugged away his touch and left the office. Matthew watched as she passed a random aisle in fiction before heading up the stairs. He didn't see what she plucked off the shelf and was fairly certain that she didn't, either.

Jack

"When things are tough, book people go back to their roots," Granddaddy Jack told his great granddaughter.

The girl was crestfallen over some injustice done at school that day. She was only six, and six-year-olds shouldn't have to bear the burdens of other people's ignorance. Yet little AJ seemed to take on that burden frequently. Jack had seen the little girl try to smooth over situations with a kind word or a gentle touch to the right person. Where Maude kept a distance from everyone's business, except for a dictator mentality she took with her own, and Sidney simply started fires wherever she went, AJ was a peacemaker, constantly putting out fires.

It was a genetically encoded trait passed down from Emma, he supposed, because she certainly hadn't gotten those traits from Maude or Sidney. He was determined to nurture AJ properly, to do right by her and make up where he'd failed the others.

"What are their roots?" Her eyes were wide and questioning, eager for information to lay away for future use.

"Words and books, of course!"

"Of course," she parroted.

He handed her a copy of Laura Ingalls Wilder's *Little House in the Big Woods.* "Start here," he said.

She was an obedient and compliant girl in all things and immediately sat in the living room to complete her assignment. So different from Sidney at that age, who would've said, "Roots are for trees!" and slipped her hand in his pockets in search of gum or candy instead.

In those days, Maude would have been around to witness the exchange and would have thrown her hands up in frustration, her inability to understand her own child evidence of Jack's failings as a father.

Matthew

Matthew crept into the upstairs office near AJ's suite. She had fallen asleep curled up in a mountain of paperwork spread across the floor.

Certified letters from lawyers, piles of bank statements and receipts—she was organizing her case. The shop, having hemorrhaged funds just to get the collection in the first place, didn't have the income to hire their own lawyers. Instead, a retired paralegal from Briar was helping them where he could.

Matthew wished she'd stop trying to do this all herself and just come to him for help. His gut told him to pick it all up and do it for her, but over the last few months, those tactics had simply annoyed her.

At first, he didn't understand how she and Sidney could possibly be related. AJ had been nothing but hard work and poise from the minute he saw her, while Sidney was all flippancy and spitfire. In times of high stress, however, it seemed they met in the middle. Sidney fled and shut everyone out. AJ disappeared, too, just within herself, shutting everyone out.

He sat down in the paperwork, just wanting to feel the silent closeness they had in the past. A letter caught his eyes, one from George Edelstein, Sr. before he died.

> *Dear Ms. Rhys,*
>
> *I would be delighted to sell you my collection upon the event of my death. Unfortunately, there will likely be a bidding war. I admired your grandfather, Jack Walters, immensely, and so I will make a special note to my lawyers regarding my preferences toward your shop. There are a few signed copies in the collection I would love to see returned "home" regardless of the estate's outcome. They are enclosed.*
>
> *George Edelstein, Sr.*

It was handwritten. The man clearly loved his books and his collection and had only ever cared that it got in the right hands. Did his son know this? Surely a son would want what his father wanted, but maybe not in all things. Matthew knew firsthand the arguments that could arise between a dad and his offspring. But for his books, for his life's work . . .

Matthew took the letter and photocopied it.

George

George received a photocopied letter posted from the Lily Hollow post office. Peculiar that it hadn't gone through the lawyers in Briar, as had the rest of the certified mail. Then again, this letter wasn't certified.

"Dear sir, I thought you would want to know your father's wishes," was chicken scratched on a Post-It note attached to the letter.

George peered at the photocopy. It was written in what was undeniably Dad's shaky handwriting.

What thieves! The cunning little bookstore clerks hadn't just weaseled the collection from his father's terminally ill fingers but already had pity-swindled copies not included in the auction manifest.

Jack Walters's first editions, nonetheless!

He did a quick Google search after realizing he had no idea who that was.

Aha! A Lily Hollow native. Surely a goldmine for the citizens of Lily Hollow!

George immediately put on a jacket and started dialing his lawyer. *Wait until they see this little piece of evidence!* The phone rang as his foot hit the pavement of the sidewalk just outside his home.

"It's more likely the courts will see this as a living will, Mr. Edelstein," the lawyer said.

George was annoyed. "Seriously? Look, he even stated there would be a bidding war. Clearly, this store cheated somehow! A little two-bit store from nowhere wins the auction of the century? No way."

The lawyer was losing patience with Edelstein. He was emotional and unreasonable. He was petulant and unhappy and just wanted to keep everyone around him unhappy, too. But the firm had worked for the Edelsteins since its beginning, and George Edelstein, Jr. paid hefty fees for his frivolous lawsuits. Of course, this hadn't been the first one. He'd been courtroom-happy long before his father's book collection was at stake. Like a hypochondriac in a hospital, Edelstein had an unhealthy love-hate relationship with the justice system and fed off the energy of a courthouse the same way an addict fed off heroin.

The lawyer thought she was about to shoot herself in the foot and probably obliterate her standing in the firm.

"George," she said. "May I call you George?"

He seemed to grunt in acquiescence. He peered at her with blood-shot eyes, the first time he'd really looked at her since they'd met.

"I think you should go visit the store."

"You—what? Lily Hollow?"

"Yes. Go. Check it out. Don't say anything. Just look around."

"Why?"

"I don't know. See if you think they're the kind of people who would swindle your dad. Call it a hunt for evidence."

"A hunt for evidence," he repeated.

"Yes. Just go sit in the shop and look around. Make some observations."

Ivy

It was Ivy who saw him first. That happened a lot, because it was her job to stand guard at the register all day. If it wasn't a tourist or gift-giving season, though, she generally found herself sketching locals with Prismacolors and had already compiled a sizable collection of portraits that looked much more gothic than the patrons might have liked.

"What do you plan to do with those?" Maude asked, peeking over the counter to see the sketchbook with far more interest than Ivy was entirely comfortable with. Maude's interests were usually followed by a line of critical observations that could leave you reeling for days, especially because she was generally both tactful and correct. "You can't sell them here. Everyone would throw a fit. There's a gallery in . . ."

That's when Ivy stopped listening and saw the man come in. She noticed him because it was too early in the morning for customers who weren't assorted "family" of some kind—AJ's family, anyway. The man stepped closer, and Ivy knew immediately that he wasn't from Lily Hollow. He didn't seem like a Briar resident, either.

She wrinkled her nose. He smelled like the city—well, looked like he smelled like city, anyway. And not her side of the city. He reeked of uptown. Uptown anywhere is all the same, and he hailed from there. The hoity-toity types that only come to bars on her side of the tracks because it would be considered ironic. To top it all off, he was too old to share that attitude from her generation.

He looked at Ivy with both surprise and skepticism. No doubt he had come looking for a quaint, small-town experience, and the first thing he saw was Ivy and her faux dreadlocks—tattered braids amongst darkly dyed, unwashed hair, made even thicker and wilder looking by the thin strips of paisley silk braided into chunks of hair on the sides of her head. Braids and curls spilled out every which way.

"Can I help you, sir?" she asked.

Maude turned to see who she was speaking to and squinted a bit. Ivy wondered if the woman was too proud to admit she needed glasses to see distance these days. The man, in a suit—what looked like an expensive one—hovered in the foyer space under the chandelier. He looked uncertain and undeniably out of place. Perhaps he and Maude could be fast friends. He seemed too proud to admit he had no idea what he was doing here. Sightseeing? Didn't realize he'd entered a bookshop and was looking for a hotel? Honest mistake, Ivy supposed.

He didn't answer her question, just raised his head high so he could have the exact air of looking down his nose at her.

"Welcome to the Bookshop Hotel. Can I help you, sir?" Matthew materialized from the direction of the café, repeating her question and saving her from the impending sarcasm that would have made its way from her mouth to the man who seemed to have lost his own.

"We have coffee, lattes, and tea if you'd like to start there." Matthew was gentle, using the voice you might use on a terrified animal, the one she often heard him use with AJ and Abigail but never with her or Sidney.

"Yes, a coffee," the man finally said. He followed Matthew to the café, and Ivy watched him like a hawk, too curious for her own good, eyes soaking him in so she could blend the exact hue of his suit into her sketchbook later. It was a deep indigo, black if you didn't know better, but definitely an indigo.

"Send them," Maude said crisply.

"What?"

"The portraits. Send them. Anonymously, if you like. To a gallery somewhere, anywhere away from here. Don't waste your talent."

Ivy marveled at the woman as she marched out the door. "Tell AJ I have Abigail today," she said as the door shut behind her.

George

George's ears pricked up when he heard the name AJ. All the legal documents said Anna J. Rhys, so he assumed AJ was the one he was dealing with.

"I'm Matthew." A solid blue coffee mug slid in front of George. "If you need anything, don't hesitate to ask."

The mug was what his mother would have called "country blue," a color that made George think of Little Bo Peep and bumpkins.

"Feel free to pick up a book to read here in the café," Matthew added. "We only charge if you walk out the door with it."

George appreciated that this younger man's name was Matthew, not Matt. "Matt" was all well and good when you were in grade school, but "Matthew" was a man's name. Like "George." Just as he thought it, he remembered his father. They'd shared the same name as adults, but when George was very young, he could remember his daddy calling him "Little Geo." As he'd gotten older, he'd learned to hate it, flushing when his father slipped and said it around his college friends. From then until now, George had forgotten what it was like to remember the pet name fondly.

His father had said it fondly, after all, in that distracted tone intellects and collectors have when their mind is 99% on their obsession and only 1% on the conversation of the moment.

Then a tiny woman emerged from the door behind the man called Matthew. She had a young face and a childish body, so small and thin. But something in her walk and her tired, distracted expression made her seem so much older. No wrinkles, she couldn't be but thirty at the most, but if she smiled, he suspected he would think she was in college still. There were circles under her eyes, and ever so subtly, a fresh cup of coffee appeared in her hands without her breathing a word, the transition from Matthew's hand to the woman's so smooth it was as if they were one being sharing limbs.

She yawned. "Oh, good morning," she said, blinking at him. "I wasn't expecting customers so early. Can I help you with anything?"

"No, Matthew has been helpful enough."

"Of course. He is that." Her hand rested a moment on Matthew's shoulder, and a wistful smiled turned the corners of his mouth. An unexpected touch. George recognized the feeling on the other man's face.

She disappeared as easily as she'd come.

"The owner," Matthew said as he wiped down the counter where George had spilled some sugar.

"Of course," George said, echoing AJ's words.

"It's an old hotel, renovated. The suites upstairs are intact and pretty nice."

"Oh, so you live here?"

"Yes. We all do. Just like apartments up there, except we share the back kitchen. We're working on getting the top-floor suites ready to take on boarders B&B style."

"Neat." George's answers were becoming more clipped as his interest grew.

Matthew seemed to sense that his voice wasn't matching his facial expression and asked him, "Would you like a tour?"

George was quiet a moment, then took a sip of his coffee to bide some time. "Hunt for evidence," the lawyer had said.

"Yes."

They started in the fiction room. Matthew explained how the place had been the grand hotel of Lily Hollow back in the day. Before that, it had been an old family estate.

"Wilbur Bartholomew James the First built her from scratch. These piers"— Matthew knocked on a pillar that went from beneath the floorboards to the balcony-like hallway of the second floor above them—"are the originals. Refurbished, of course, but they've been here from the start of it all."

Matthew seemed so proud, you'd have thought he was Wilbur Bartholomew James himself in the flesh.

"Let me guess, he's your grandfather."

"Oh, no," Matthew said. "My family is from Texas. No, James passed it to his son, who then sold it to Jack Walters."

"Jack Walters, the author?"

"Well, yes. I always forget he was an author. He was AJ's great grandfather—the woman, the owner you met."

"Yes."

"She inherited the building. It was pretty run down when she got it and fixed it up and started a bookstore. She's real big into family legacies."

George felt his eyebrows rise. "Is she?"

"Absolutely. Come, I'll show you something really cool." Matthew ushered George to a side room—toward the back, actually. There was a window facing the back of the property, and the gardens looked extensive. The room was lined with mahogany shelves, much nicer than the shelves in the rest of the shop. Velvet wing-backed chairs faced each other, sharing a tall coffee table shockingly similar to one in his father's library.

"What is this?" George asked, waving his hands.

"It's a room we're turning into a rare and antiquities room." Matthew pointed to a bronze plaque on the wall. "We're not supposed to reveal it until a gala we're having, but . . ." Matthew trailed off as George stepped closer to read the plaque.

"The George Edelstein Room, dedicated to the greatest bibliophile of our time." His father's birth year and death year were under the dedication: 1936-2013.

George felt a choke rising in his throat. "The collection is going to stay all together? Not sold off?"

"For the most part. There are a few pieces being auctioned off to cover costs. The collection put us in the hole a great deal. But a few of the pieces to the right auctions and museums should keep us afloat. Then some of the lesser pieces are to go to auction the night of the gala to keep the old hotel patrons tied to the place. A feel-good auction, so to speak.

"But for the most part, AJ wanted to keep it together to honor the legacy of Edelstein and collectors like him the best she could. We'd rather pull more visitors to Lily Hollow, to the Hotel itself, than sell off all the pieces. We can sell later printings and coffee if we keep people in the door, to pay the bills. This room, hopefully, will be bigger than us. Bigger than the bills."

"Yes." George choked again. "I'm sure Edelstein would have liked that."

Matthew nodded, apparently done speaking for the day after his pretty speech.

"Can I see the upstairs?" George asked.

Sidney

The night before, a text had popped up on Sidney's cell: "They are moving Abby to Maude's. Could use help." It was Ivy who had sent the text. Sidney had smiled. She missed her young friend, a girl young enough to be a second daughter, but someone she had discovered the ability to pursue an untainted relationship with.

Sid threw her suitcase and purse into the Mercedes and sat in the driver's seat. She rested her head on the steering wheel. It was time. It was time to stop hiding out in Briar. She was ready to go home and face everyone. She wasn't a runner, not anymore. She was prepared to stay in Lily Hollow forever if that's what her friends and family wanted. It didn't feel like giving up her dreams anymore. It felt like realizing her dreams could be different than she'd supposed. Better. That maybe there was more to life than running.

It felt like being there for her daughter and this amazing event she was so wrapped up in planning. Helping her build healthy relationships where Sidney hadn't even known how to before. It felt like making up for misdeeds. It felt like not being selfish.

The old man at that coffee shop was right. She'd regret what she missed, and ultimately, she had to make a choice as to what was worth missing and what must be fought for. The freedom to gallivant, she'd done that already. She didn't want to miss out on having a real home and being welcome there. She didn't want to burn her bridges. She wanted to travel on all those bridges and bask in real, loving relationships. Even if Sam didn't want her anymore, she didn't want to miss finding out. Even if he wasn't meant for her, she didn't want to miss out on seeing him happy.

She didn't want to miss seeing AJ happy, either. Or her new friend, Ivy. She didn't want to miss Abby's last years. She didn't want to miss out on getting to know her own mother.

Sid wanted to be here. Well, not *here* here. She looked up at the town home in the center of town that served as the Briar Bed & Breakfast where she'd been staying. But she wanted to be in this neck of the world. She wanted to be in Lily Hollow. It sounded strange even thinking that. Lily Hollow had always been what she ran from, and now she was dying to get back. Instinctively, she scratched her thigh. That itch reminding her of what it felt like when she abandoned a path.

She turned the key in the ignition, and the engine started. She put the car in reverse and saw the old man, cane in hand, heading toward the edge of the square. He stepped off the road and crossed the ditch, heading to the woods, it seemed. She swung the car around, and he looked her way and gave her a little wave. *Thank you*, she thought, waving back.

On the highway toward Lily Hollow, she was relaxed, when years ago she would have tensed up. The trees just off the shoulder and the bends in the road that used to make her cringe, each one a well-known landmark noting her estimated time of arrival, now brought a bit of joy. She passed MacGregor's Farms and the market and drove until the large wooden sign buried in lilies loomed over her. *Entering Lily Hollow.* And she thought, *How lovely. How beautiful.* The car merged onto Swan Lane, and Sidney thought, *You really do see what you want to see.*

Matthew

"They dropped the suit!" AJ burst out. She tore out of the office, startling Matthew, as AJ wasn't the sort of person prone to outbursts. His heart surged, not for the news as much as for the fact that finally, she had shared an emotion and invited him to join.

"They dropped it! Out of nowhere! The gala is saved!" She waved a letter in his face. He took it from her gently and read it before looking back at her. This would make everything better. This was the answer to all his prayers and everything he needed.

He smiled broadly. Ivy jumped on the register counter and started dancing. AJ shot her a look but couldn't stop smiling herself. He knew the idea of Ivy on the antique counter grated on her but didn't matter in the grand scheme of their news. This affected everyone affiliated with the bookstore. This affected all of Lily Hollow, whether they knew it or not. This was the moment they'd all been hoping for. Matthew found AJ in his arms, and they celebrated by hugging it out while Ivy continued to gyrate on the counter.

The wind chimes above the double doors tinkled, signaling someone entering the hotel. Nancy put her well-manicured hands on her pink hips and said, "Well, I never. Ivy!"

"They dropped the suit, Nancy," Matthew said. He didn't get all the words out of his mouth before Nancy squealed like a sorority sister and clapped her hands.

"The gala is saved!"

"The gala is saved," he repeated and kissed AJ's forehead.

AJ's face calmed, and her brow furrowed. "I wonder what changed."

"Does it matter?" he asked her.

"No, I guess not."

Matthew turned to see that Nancy had offered her hand to Ivy, who joined her on the floor. The two continued to dance it out while Nancy sang about twinkle lights and clean white linens and how she knew her dreams of gala grandeur could never be truly threatened.

"We've got a lot of books to process," AJ said, pulling away from Matthew and holding him at a distance for a moment without losing his gaze. "Oh my God, so many books." He could tell the overwhelming project to be tackled excited her rather than frustrated her. There, there was his AJ. He smiled again, flashing teeth in a way he didn't often do.

"Yes," he nodded, still smiling. "We've got a lot of work to do."

"I've—"

"Got the books, and I've got the coffee."

"Yes."

The two separated, and Matthew went to the kitchen to start brewing and preparing for the all-nighter he knew they were about to pull. AJ disappeared into the work room and started unpacking boxes she'd been afraid to touch.

The Edelstein collection was theirs, the gala was on, AJ had a project that energized rather than drained her, and everything was as it should be. While he waited for the water to heat up, Matthew leaned against the café counter and watched Nancy and Ivy. They were so excited about the news, they didn't see Sidney sneak past without a word. Matthew nodded to her, and she pursed her lips to him and disappeared to her room upstairs.

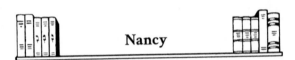

Nancy

Nancy had borrowed long tables from the high school and set them up in rows along the Green. Each one was covered in a beautiful white tablecloth and featured a guest book at one end and photo albums in between centerpieces down the length of the table. The centerpieces went along with the rest of AJ's décor, white roses and purple orchids with a large, red hibiscus in the center.

The anthers and stigma of the flowers had been removed to make room for tea light candles that made the red petals glow delicately. Beautiful white tablecloths suspiciously similar to the ones from AJ's wedding were draped beneath Nancy's handiwork. The albums had place settings with the year and were lined up in chronological order so a person could walk a physical timeline of the Lily Hollow Hotel.

Everything was set under huge white tents, like the photograph AJ had shown her—a typical, traditional, outdoor Lily Hollow wedding. Many of the guests tonight would tear up at the sight of it. White lights were draped along the posts and through the rafters. She'd managed to find some very lightweight chandeliers to hang from the highest beams of the tent to give it that roaring twenties appeal. There was still room for the band AJ had hired at the end of the Green closest to the double doors of the Hotel.

It was beautiful, and she began to tear up herself. *Excellent work, Nancy Harrigan*, she congratulated herself. She wiped her eyes dry before anyone noticed and poured a glass of champagne right there at the end of the table. It was still early and bright outside, but she was sure guests would be arriving soon. They were the sort of crowd to come early, not fashionably late.

The band AJ had brought in was, in reality, a motley crew of random musicians from the college in Briar. Apparently, a few of them played together in coffee shops and student gatherings around town, but AJ had given them set lists and told them to remember to keep it nostalgic. Like the timeline on the tables, the musicians would be playing instrumental pieces from throughout the hotel's history. Light jazz from parties past as guests arrived, pieces from wedding marches long ago, and by the time they were heading out, a Michael Bolton cover.

Nancy was pleased. She knew the acoustics of the Green and the surrounding woods well. The music would be heard in the circle drive and would be subtle background noise during the dinner and party inside. There was a lone violinist stationed in the gardens where sounds from the front could not reach.

Nancy took a chair, kicked off her pink heels, and clasped her hands around her champagne glass.

"Perfect," Sam said as he walked the last trays of hors d'oeuvre from the deli.

Sam

Sam looked through the tents to the front porch where Sidney stood looking like a red pillar of fire, with all white and crystal in the foreground. She didn't see him, and he watched her scoop up a flower and push it into her hair.

If you were to somehow be blind to the Green, the front porch of the Bookshop Hotel made the enormity of this event unmistakable. Lights and white roses with purple orchids and red flowers, whose name escaped Sam for a moment, twined around each pillar and seemed to race up onto the arches from the roof of the porch. All the lights of the Hotel were on, floor to attic, and as late afternoon turned into evening, the sight would blow anyone away.

White lights draped throughout the branches of the two trees closest to the old building, and a red carpet had been laid out down the porch steps where Sidney stood in crystal shoes like Cinderella. Where in hell had the woman found crystal shoes?

Sidney plucked a white rose from the post closest to her, and Sam was just about to roll his eyes at her presumption of stealing not one but two flowers from the décor when he saw her turn and nestle the rose into Abigail's hair. Sam softened. It seemed as though Sidney was Abigail's date for the evening, and the old woman was a breathtaking version of herself in an old-fashioned yellow dress.

Ivy appeared at Abigail's other arm wearing the green dress Sidney had picked out for their wedding. He was surprised how natural Ivy looked in it and was even more surprised that Sidney had let her wear it. Sidney wasn't one to share her carefully selected clothing with others, and this dress was even more carefully selected. Sam didn't know what to think. It was a testament to how much Sidney had grown and a sure sign that all bets were off when it came to them being together, or at least of her hanging her hopes on a wedding that year.

Peter

Peter stood on the Green of the Hotel. He had only been here once in his whole life and somehow had ended up on the guest list for this gala. He had looked over the invitation a million times. It wasn't in Abigail's handwriting, but then again, who could say he remembered it properly?

The invitation was worded in such a way that implied he had been a patron of the hotel. It had been so long ago, he had forgotten why someone would think that. How would anyone have known he had ever set foot in its door? Then he remembered the guestbook on the podium in the lobby. He had signed it so as to look like he belonged there, as though he had a purpose. Really, he had just known Abigail might be around, and he had come to spy on her. He'd heard her voice coming from an office, and she'd sounded agitated. He could tell her entire mood from just the sound of her voice, and this one was not a relaxed mood.

Jack Walters had emerged from the office, eyed him, and disappeared out the doors. He knew it was Jack from the paperback novels at the library. Abigail had mentioned him in passing once, and after that awkward day in the woods, he had done some research.

A girl had popped out of the kitchen with a cookie in her mouth. She was young but tall like her father. "Daddy," she said.

Jack was already gone, and Abigail came out to greet the girl. Peter was suddenly shy, out of Briar, out of his depth and the reality in which he knew Abigail, and he half turned his back. This wasn't going as he'd expected, and he felt foolish for being here. Everything about being here was utterly wrong.

For a brief moment, he suspected this child of being Abigail's, the way the girl responded to her when she said, "Come on, Maude. Let's go to the bakery." Abigail was so focused on the little girl, she didn't see Peter, and he felt a relief rush over him. His folly would not be found out.

Standing in front of the old building now was different, yet the same. This wasn't a quiet afternoon, and he was here by invitation, not by stealth. But he still eyed an unsuspecting Abigail, and she was still oblivious to him. He wasn't alone. His grandchildren lurked about, not interested in the gala itself, but in the George Edelstein Collection.

She looked like a dream in that yellow dress. They were both old, he knew that—so old, she might not even recognize him. After all, it had been so many years since they'd set eyes on each other. But there she was, looking like a little piece of heaven.

Maybe she'd made the right choice all those years ago. He'd had a happy life. He loved his wife until the day she died. His children were his pride and joy, and he couldn't imagine things any differently. His grandchildren were smart and caring, all good people. Abigail's choice in the woods so long ago had led him toward this legacy, this happiness, this life. Still, ever so briefly, as he saw her there in yellow, a bit flowerlike and breezy under the twinkle lights, he wondered what his life and legacy would have looked like if she'd joined him.

His granddaughter tugged his arm ever so slightly to urge him to the tables under the tent on the Green. He let her guide him to them, allowing her to believe he was part of the history there even though he knew he wasn't. He skimmed the old photos, feigning an interest when all he wanted to do was take another peek at the lovely lady in yellow on the front porch. He remembered their long walks in the woods and missed her with an aching pain that defied reason, and suddenly, he wished he wasn't an old man. He wished he was younger, walking those woods with Abigail.

He looked up from the albums laid out on the tables. "Look, Granddad. Look at this," his granddaughter was saying, but he was looking out from the tables at her.

He remembered the way she looked with her hair splayed out over grass under rays of sunlight. He remembered being so certain he had met her for the sole purpose of one day being her husband and loving her forever. But now he saw that he'd met her for now, for this reason. To be the one to witness her old and remember her young. To be the one who thought she was just as beautiful, even if it was a different kind of beauty altogether, as someone on the verge of heaven rather than someone on the verge of what they considered middle age back then.

"I'm sorry, darling. I'd like to go this way." He patted his granddaughter's hand. She looked startled, but she complied and he led her toward the porch. Abigail was sitting now on a chair with a young woman holding her hand as well.

When he stood in front of her, he longed to stoop at her knee, but he was too old to bend that way. It had been years since his legs had allowed him to move the way he liked. Instead, he hunched a little.

"I'm here to see Abigail," he said.

She had already been looking up, but now he saw that she just barely recognized her name and was grasping at his. Her eyes were ever wistful, lost in some thought or memory that Peter was not privy to and never had been. It seemed the way things had always been with them, her there with him physically but off in her own world mentally.

"Peter."

This was what his granddaughter had expected would happen. This was nothing like what Sidney and AJ had expected. Who was Peter? How did Abigail know him?

"You know this man, Abigail?" Sidney asked.

"Oh, yes. This is my best friend, Peter. Peter, this is Jack's . . ." For a moment, Abigail had been lucid, but Peter could tell she had lost her train of thought when she glanced over at Sidney, seemingly unable to remember the woman's relation to Jack.

"I'm Sidney." She put out her hand to the man. "I'm Jack Walters's granddaughter. My daughter owns the Hotel now and put this together."

"I see," Peter said with a nod.

"Let me go get more chairs," Sidney said after shaking his hand.

He took Sidney's chair and sat next to Abigail. His granddaughter turned to survey the party, leaning against a carefully lit pillar.

Abigail reached for his hand. "Peter, I've missed you."

"And I you, Abigail."

She tilted her head to his shoulder and let her body lean into him. He'd thought of this moment often over the years, what it would feel like to have her next to him, holding hands. She was always so sturdy and strong back then, and that was how he'd always remembered her. Now she was frail. He supposed he was, too. She didn't smell of the outdoors anymore, either, but it seemed she'd never stopped using whatever soap it was that made her scent so familiar.

They didn't speak. They didn't have to. She'd called him her best friend, and he loved that he held that title. He hadn't known that before. He always thought it was Jack she thought of when it came to that. But he supposed that over the years, perhaps Jack had become more of an obligation than a friend. Or perhaps Jack would always be more than a friend to her. Who knew? Only Abigail.

It didn't matter. He held her hand in his, and the whole evening was worth it. Putting on this suit was worth it. Having his grandchildren fuss over him for a week when all he wanted to do was sit in his garden in peace . . . this made it all worth it.

"I'm glad it's you here, in the end," Abigail said. "I'll be gone soon, you know."

He nodded, and a tear came to his eyes. He'd become quite the teary-eyed gentleman in his old age, something that bothered him greatly in his fifties but now didn't matter.

"I love you, Abigail."

"I love you, too, Peter."

The granddaughter moved to accept a glass of wine off a tray. Sidney had appeared with chairs but placed them on the other side of the porch, not wanting to disturb the two old friends and their moment. They were silent, but the two old souls were communicating.

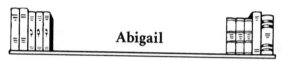

Abigail

The night seemed a little like heaven. She was wearing her yellow dress, one that should have been lost to time and dust moths but instead was as cheerful as the first day she put it on. Jack wasn't there. He was gone. Sometimes, she remembered that. Sometimes, she lost track of why he was missing. When this happened, she looked down to her hands—old and weathered, knotted a bit with age—and remembered.

Folded there in her lap, she could see the tiniest of white flowers imbedded in the material under her fingers. You could only see them up close. From far away, the dress was a simple, solid, pale yellow. She remembered the day the dress was pulled from the box, shipped from somewhere, ordered from some special catalog. Evie had always loved catalogs. All those books that Jack passed their way when they were girls—only Abigail had ever known the truth.

Evie never really read them. She'd skim a few pages, close the book, and cast it aside on her bed with disdain. Sometimes, she would speculate momentarily what it was Jack wanted to hear about it. Often times, she'd choose a character to adore or hate despite knowing little about them. Usually, she just pulled out a magazine and surveyed the pictures. Fashion and shopping catalogs, that was the truth behind Evie. Evie would never admit to such a thing, being such an ordinary trait in a girl, so normal and so typical, and Evie didn't like the idea of being normal or typical.

Abigail looked up from her lap. Sidney was beside her, looking so lovely and calm. She'd done what Evie never could. Sidney had faced those demons of hers head-on and won. Evie had seen the slightest glimpse of her demons and folded in defeat. Where was Evie? On the other side, waiting? What was the forever after going to be like? Maybe a bit like this.

Abigail looked beyond the porch to the twinkle lights on the Green. She could hear the rustle of people just inside the Hotel through the windows behind her, pressing to see the George Edelstein Collection before all was revealed. The soft lights and the sounds of humanity were calming to her.

A man interrupted her thoughts. It was a man she knew, a man she loved. She felt Sidney take a step back with a little gasp.

"You," Sidney said.

"Hello, dear. I've come to see Abigail." Peter reached his hand out to Abigail's, and she smiled and said his name.

It had been lovely seeing him again. Even lovelier still for the two of them to watch hand-in-hand as Sam found Sidney, as they kissed and made up, as they committed to be what they were always meant to be. It was no wedding, not yet, but it was the beginning of a marriage. Abigail could see the intention between them, that they were finally both on the same page and ready to face life as partners.

She was happy about that. Abigail only wanted what she'd always wanted, for Jack's children—for all his girls—to find peace with themselves. All she had ever needed was for her chosen family to discover what her biological family had never acquired: harmony and grace.

Maude took Abigail's hand from Peter when it got late in the night, long after the Edelstein ceremony. Edelstein's son had even stood up and made a toast to the crowd, thanking them for their interest in his father's life's passions. Things were winding down now; it was all ending. Sidney was cleaning up with Sam, folding up tablecloths that would need to be laundered.

Heather was packing up serving trays from the baked goods that were served. She assured Abigail that she would handle washing them, no need to come to the bakery any earlier than usual. Matthew was collapsing tables with Nancy on the Green, and AJ was standing in the midst of it all in her gorgeous dress, looking a bit like a lost bride at the end of her own reception.

"Are you okay to walk, Abigail?" Maude asked.

"I'm fit as a fiddle." Abigail held tightly to the offered fingers, and the two ladies picked their way gingerly through all the debris of a successful gala. Once on Main Street, she looked back. Peter had found his grandchildren, and they were getting into their car. He looked to Abigail, and they waved a last farewell to each other.

Back in Jack Walters's home—no, it was all Maude's now—the yellow dress came off, a nightgown dropped over her head. For the first time, Maude did what Abigail had done for her thousands of times when she was small. She tucked her into bed, pressing the comforter around the woman until her eyes drifted shut.

Maude kissed the woman's cheek, admitting to herself that Abigail was possibly the only mother she'd ever remember clearly. What would she be without this woman? What would Sidney be? And AJ? Abigail had always been the glue that held them all together. She'd always been a little resentful of Abigail for her warmth with Sidney and AJ—a warmth Maude could never find in herself—but now she was grateful for it. Finally, Maude felt blessed by it. Maude stood and left the sleeping woman to her dreams, closing the door ever so softly behind her.

Abigail never woke up.

AJ

AJ thought she could go the rest of her life without ever seeing another lawyer again. Jude had promised her college money when she was small but, of course, hadn't honored that promise. And instead of telling her himself, he'd sent his lawyer. Great dad, that one.

She'd been visited by insurance lawyers after Kevin's death, mostly wanting to discover whether he had purposely crashed the car, as she suspected he had. She'd kept her mouth shut. Then all this business with George Edelstein. Thank God all that was over and the books were nestled happily in the rare book room.

Now Abigail was gone, and who knew—the old bird had a will.

AJ's mother's voice broke her thoughts. "She gave me what?"

"An estate," the lawyer repeated.

"Abigail had an estate?" Sidney was flabbergasted.

"A castle in the woods . . ." AJ whispered.

Maude clasped her hand over her mouth, a memory of cast iron gates and a fountain tugging at the corners of her mind.

"Why me?" Sidney asked.

The lawyer looked puzzled. Why would he know? Why complain? It was free land.

Maude

When Maude heard that Sidney inherited an estate from Abigail, she gasped. Immediately, she knew what estate, and immediately, visions of cast iron and her weeping father entered her mind. Why would Abigail do that? Why would Abigail leave something with their family that had caused so much pain?

They loaded up into Sam's truck at first, but, coming up on Mac-Gregor Bridge, changed their minds and decided to walk. The bridge was suspect, Maude told them, so all of them poured out of the car together and walked the rest of the way. Traipsing through the woods with the map of the property the lawyer had given them, they wound their way along the road. It was in honor of Abigail, if nothing else, and they filled it with stories of her and speculation as to what she had been hiding out in the woods for so many years.

Maude remained silent, holding her breath for most of their trek, afraid to see what she knew she would see when they came upon the property.

"Why do you think she left it to me?" Sidney asked again and again. Sam kept shrugging, and Maude kept asking the same thing in her head.

"I suppose," Sam said, "she figured Jack gave AJ the hotel, I own the house, you needed a chunk of land in the woods . . . ?" His voice trailed off into a question.

No one needed this land out in the woods. No one. But it was true, they all had a piece of something that was important to Abigail, all except Sidney. Maude supposed it made sense that Sidney would get the discarded parts, the parts that reminded them they all had a little bit of darkness to hide. "We were her children," Maude agreed, "and she knew I wouldn't want it."

"Why not, Mom?" Sidney asked.

Maude looked around and walked her fingers along the stone. She looked up into the face of the statue in the fountain. How could anyone want to own that face? It was the face that had always terrified her. It was Abigail's, but evil. It was Evie's, the name emerging into the forefront of her mind, but slightly different. Because it was there, etched in stone?

How could anyone want any of this? Unless they needed to feel like they had a place to escape to, a place they probably wouldn't actually visit but just know was there. Maude slowly began to understand.

"That statue looks a lot like Abigail," Sidney said.

"No, Abigail was prettier," Maude snapped a bit and then corrected herself gently. "Kinder, I mean."

"Well, like you said, Sam. You have the house, AJ has the Hotel . . . What do I do with it?" Sidney sat on the ledge of the circular concrete fountain, seemingly taking in the crumbling wall, the overgrown ivy, and the tall grass everywhere.

Maude sat with her daughter and patted her hand, awkwardly at first, and then settling into the sensation when Sidney didn't pull away.

"What do you want to do with it?" Maude asked, realizing she'd probably never actually asked Sidney what she wanted about anything, not without a tone of dictatorship that was meant to guide her to a decision. She saw the surprise in Sidney's face, and briefly, it hurt her feelings that Sidney's expression only confirmed her own realization.

"I have no idea. You and AJ are the big planners."

AJ ran her hands along a doorway—daydreaming, no doubt—with Matthew not far behind trying to read her expression. Sidney and Maude both saw this at the same time and laughed a bit.

"I think I'll just let it come to me," Sidney said, and Maude knew that Abigail had done perfectly.

"So many possibilities." Maude nudged her daughter.

"Yes." Sidney smiled. "Possibilities."

Maude stood, dusted off the seat of her slacks, and turned away from the estate. The face of that woman turned her stomach, but the well-being of her daughter made her glad.

Abigail had known that all Sidney really needed was a place she felt she could escape to. Even if she never ventured there, she would feel less restless knowing it was there. The child struggled when she felt trapped, but offer her the world and she'd figure out the right path in the long run.

Maybe that's what Daddy had meant for her all along, but instead of telling her she *could* go, he'd told her *to* go. Abigail knew Jack had only gotten it half right, and now Maude saw all the orchestrating and puppeteering the two had attempted through the years.

Maude drank in the sight of the stone and the ivy, avoiding the face. Such a shame. It would have made for a lovely place to sketch if that woman wasn't lording over the property like an evil moon goddess.

Maude pushed her hair out of her face. There was sweat on her brow and upper lip from the excursion, but she felt a chill as she walked back to the bridge where the car was waiting. It was nice to close this chapter of her life once and for all. The puzzle pieces had all found their resting places. Now she was ready to go home and not think of any of it again. She was too old to be fearful of ghosts any longer.

A kitten slinked across the bridge, a brownish-red color instead of a typical orange tabby. Maude looked around to see if there was a mother and a litter nearby. Sometimes, the feral cats of Lily Hollow found themselves here to breed. She went to pick him up, and he moved to scratch her but thought better of it. She scooped him up, and he purred against her chest. He was hungry.

Henry. She thought of him instantly and missed him. It had been so long, she was used to his absence and even more used to not thinking of him from day to day. Once, before he left the last time, he'd said, "You should get a cat to keep you company." It was off hand, and she'd never followed up on the offer. Sidney came, life happened, she had no use for pets.

"Henry."

The cat purred.

"What did you find?" AJ asked her as she and Matthew climbed into Sam's truck.

"It's a cat, isn't that obvious?" Maude frowned at her granddaughter.

"You're keeping him?"

"Well, what does it look like?"

AJ just smiled at Maude as she scooted into the front seat.

"And I'm naming him after your grandfather," Maude added.

"Jack?" AJ asked.

"No, not my daddy. My husband, Henry. Your actual grandfather."

Sam

"Let's go home," Sam said.

"Yes, let's. Would you like to walk with me?"

"I would." Sam passed the keys off to AJ and took Sidney's hand. Not long after they walked through the old iron gates and found themselves on the road, AJ and Matthew pulled out behind them in Sam's truck.

"You sure you're walking?" Matthew asked, leaning out the window.

The couple nodded together in calm agreement and continued their journey home as the sound of the vehicle made its way into the distance and out of earshot. They passed the fork in the road and turned toward Lily Hollow, away from the MacGregor Woods. They came upon the MacGregor Bridge.

"I'm glad you're coming home with me," Sam said.

"Me, too. It's spooky out here."

A breeze trickled through the trees and swept over them as they stood on the bridge. The water burbled beneath them over rocks. A fish made a splash.

Sam eyed Sidney with unguarded love and respect. He took in her red hair, always so much like his, but darker. For a moment, he imagined her as she was long ago, chewing bubble gum, yellow plastic earrings clanking against her cheek. Even out here in the woods with no makeup or earrings, a little disturbed by the sound of the fish and eerie feeling of the bridge, Sam couldn't help but think she was pretty—prettier than she'd ever been.

Acknowledgments

My personal editor and co-author Katie Lavois, who makes everything readable before my publisher sees it.

The editors at Grey Gecko Press for being the kind of grammar Nazis necessary for publishing quality work.

Danielle, Emily, and JJ, my friends and sisters in Christ.

Half Price Books (Humble) and Good Books in the Woods. I wouldn't be a writer without the existence of these two wonderful bookstores.

The Bookshop Hotel fans, because this book would not have happened without your support.

Adam Jones and Julie McKay, for letting me join their writing group.

The Woodlands Social Ride (bike club) who were my weekly connection to the world when I was writing this book.

About the Author

A.K. Klemm lives in Texas with her husband, daughter, and hounds. *The Bookshop Hotel* series is an ode to her years spent at Half Price Books in Humble and one of her favorite stores, Good Books in the Woods.

She is a wife, a mother, a dog lover, a retired bookseller and buyer from a used bookstore, a third degree black belt and martial arts instructor, forager, aspiring cyclist, a Christian, a sister, an aunt, a college graduate, a movie making enthusiast, and . . . oh yeah, a bibliomaniac.

Connect with A. K.

Email:	andiklemm@rocketmail.com
Facebook:	facebook.com/AnakalianWhims
Web:	anakalianwhims.wordpress.com
Twitter:	@ AnakalianWhims

Grey Gecko Press

Thank you for reading this book from Grey Gecko Press, an independent publishing company bringing you great books by your favorite new indie authors.

Be one of the first to hear about new releases from Grey Gecko: visit our website and sign up for our New Release or All-Access email lists. Don't worry: we hate spam, too. You'll only be notified when there's a new release, we'll never share your email with anyone for any reason, and you can unsubscribe at any time.

At our website you can purchase all our titles, including special and autographed editions, preorder upcoming books, and find out about two great ways to get free books, the Slushpile Reader Program and the Advance Reader Program.

And don't forget: all our print editions come with the ebook free!

www.GreyGeckoPress.com

Support Indie Authors & Small Press

If you liked this book, please take a few moments to leave a review on your favorite website, even if it's only a line or two. Reviews make all the difference to indie authors and are one of the best ways you can help support our work.

Reviews on Amazon, GreyGeckoPress.com, GoodReads, Barnes and Noble, or even on your own blog or website all help to spread the word to more readers about our books, and nothing's better than word-of-mouth!

http://smarturl.it/review-lilyhollow

Recommended Reading

Chickens & Hens
by Nancy-Gail Burns

When young Marnie unexpectedly loses her father, her grandmother moves into her home to help her mother and all three women must create a new life together—all while Marnie goes through the trials of adolescence in 1960s small-town America.

Marnie witnesses unexpected lessons—from the heartwarming to the hilarious—learned by family and townsfolk. She also sees the older women in her life fall in love again. But will Marnie ever find true love herself... or has she missed the most important lesson of all?

Find out in this delightful story of three women who will make you laugh, make you cry, and above all, make you proud to be a woman.

amazon iBooks   grey gecko press
BARNES&NOBLE kobo   http://bit.ly/1qFTGye
BOOKSELLERS

Seashells, Gator Bones, and the Church of Everlasting Liability
Stories from a Small Florida Town in the 1930s

by Susan Adger

In the 1930s, the fictional town of Toad Springs, Florida, is filled with the adventures and daily whatnots of worthy, down-to-earth folk such as Flavey Stroudamore, owner of a three-legged gator named Precious who also just happens to have a birthmark of Jesus on his side.

Joining Flavey are Buck Blander, pastor of the Church of Everlasting Liability, who honed his preaching skills in prison but doesn't tell his parishioners, and Sweetie Mooney, whose attempt to run a beauty shop in her aunt's home fails after tragedies with head lice and henna hair dye.

This lively, heartwarming collection of tales from the Sunshine State will inspire you to smile!

amazon iBooks   grey gecko press
BARNES&NOBLE kobo   http://bit.ly/Y4lTLc
BOOKSELLERS

CPSIA information can be obtained at www.ICGtesting.com
Printed in the USA
BVOW08s2329190816

459525BV00002B/22/P